DEATH OF A SAFEBREAKER

A 1930s country house mystery

Peter Zander-Howell

Copyright © 2024 Peter Zander-Howell

All rights reserved.

Certain well-known historical persons are mentioned in this work. All other characters and events portrayed in this book are fictitious, and any similarity to real persons, alive or dead, is coincidental and not intended by the author. Real-world locations in this book may have been slightly altered.

No part of this book may be reproduced, or stored in a retrieval system, or transmitted in any form or by any means, electronic, mechanical, photocopying, recording, or otherwise, without the express permission of the publisher.

Cover image © Alamy

CONTENTS

Title Page	
Copyright	
List of characters:	1
CHAPTER 1	3
CHAPTER 2	10
CHAPTER 3	16
CHAPTER 4	23
CHAPTER 5	29
CHAPTER 6	41
CHAPTER 7	52
CHAPTER 8	68
CHAPTER 9	78
CHAPTER 10	90
CHAPTER 11	96
CHAPTER 12	101
CHAPTER 13	111
CHAPTER14	116

CHAPTER 15	132
CHAPTER16	143
CHAPTER 17	150
CHAPTER 18	161
CHAPTER 19	173
CHAPTER 20	187
CHAPTER 21	191
CHAPTER 22	201
Books By This Author	211

LIST OF CHARACTERS:

The Family:

Edgar, 1st Viscount Tallis of Wythall
The Hon. Walter Tallis, and his wife Jill
The Hon. Pat Burgess, and her husband Cornelius
The Hon. Charity Carey, and her husband Norman
The Hon. Emily Starling, and her husband Craig

The Guests:

Mr Maurice Todd – invited by Emily
Miss Cissie Saunders – invited by Craig
Mrs Cora McBride – invited by Norman
The Hon. Bruce Leach – invited by Charity
Mr Eustace Beaumont – invited by Walter
Mr Jonathan Payne – invited by Cornelius

Some of the Wythall Staff:

Mr Herbert Partridge (Butler)
Mrs Julia Hobbs (Housekeeper)
Mrs Sarah Green (Cook)
Mr John Pettit (Footman
Miss Lizzie Wells (Parlourmaid)
Miss Agnes Johns (Parlourmaid)
Miss Beatrix ('Trixie') Church (Parlourmaid)
Mr Frank Mason (Footman)
Mr Percy Talbot (Boot boy)

Other characters:

Mr Meredith Hammond (Lord Tallis's right-hand man)
Dr Bailey (Local GP)
Dr Gifford (Police Surgeon)

Police officers from the Worcestershire Constabulary:

Detective Inspector Tommy Rees
Detective Sergeant Knowles
Police Constable Pardoe
Superintendent Foster
Colonel Meadows (The Chief Constable)

The Deceased:

Mr Daniel Skinner

CHAPTER 1

Use of the expression 'pitch dark' by a speaker or author will often be hyperbole. Coal tar pitch being one of the blackest things in the natural world, it was perhaps unsurprising that the adjective came into the English-speaking world to describe an absence of light. In reality, few situations have total darkness. But some do.

For the watcher inside the study, it was indeed pitch dark. There was no light source inside the room – not even the luminous hands of a clock or watch. Heavy curtains, with generous overlaps, covered the widows. Even if they had been opened, it would have made very little difference. Outside, at one o'clock in the morning in early January, very heavy snow clouds completely covered the sky, and the minimal reflected light from a brand-new moon could not have filtered through them. No snow had yet fallen, so the ground itself was dark. The big house was half a mile from any other habitation, and even if a neighbour had been awake, it was doubtful if any light would have made a difference. On the nearest public road a similar distance away, no vehicle lights had passed for over an hour.

It was not totally silent, as a mantel clock

ticked away quietly. Normally, no one in the room would have noticed the sound, but in the stillness it now seemed very loud.

In a deeply recessed corner of the study, the watcher waited patiently, seated in a comfortable chair placed specially for this vigil.

At twenty minutes to two, the silence was broken by a faint scratching sound from the window. The watcher guessed that a diamond cutter and sucker pad were being used to remove a section of glass. A little later there was a faint click as the French window was opened. The curtain was pushed aside. The watcher sensed rather than saw this, as the light level didn't noticeably alter. The door was reclosed, almost silently, and the curtain closed again. A moment later, the darkness was pierced by the light from an electric torch, the beam pointing well away from the watcher. It briefly roamed over the floor between its owner and the far wall. Detecting no obstructions in the way, the torch seemed to move across the room. The end point appeared to be the wall safe at that end of the room.

A casual observer, had one been present, might have deduced at least two things:
First, that the watcher had certainly anticipated – had perhaps even known – that the intruder would come. Second, that this person was up to no good.

Both assumptions would obviously have been correct. In fact, the only uncertainty demonstrated by the watcher earlier was to wonder whether the man breaking in would risk switching on an electric light. As a precaution against that – which would have made it almost certain that the watcher would be seen – the bulbs had been removed from both standard lamps and from the desk lamp. There were no ceiling light fittings.

In fact, the second person, now kneeling down in front of the safe, and quite clearly intending to open it, had made no attempt to turn on the lights. The hand-held torch was set down on the floor, and the burglar put down a small bag beside it. There were faint sounds as the bag was opened. Seconds later another torch – apparently attached to the safebreaker's head like a coal miner's lamp – was switched on. The original torch was switched off. The watcher, some twenty-five feet away, could also just about pick out that the man had produced two more items, presumably from the bag – a stethoscope and a pad of paper.

Adjusting his position to be a little more comfortable, the man began twisting the dial of the combination lock.

The watcher knew the principles of the task being undertaken. The first and crucial step was to ascertain the combination length – how many wheels or 'tumblers' the safe possessed. This was likely to be three, but could be any number from two to six, and neither the watcher nor the safebreaker was in possession of this information.

The latter, however, was a professional, and

knew exactly how to determine it. It took him only a few minutes to confirm that there were three numbers, which is what he had expected when first eying the safe. He gave a barely audible sigh of relief. The next step, much more lengthy and requiring the drawing of a graph, was to determine those numbers.

Because manufacturers typically allowed a margin of error of plus or minus two on the dial, the next stage meant listening at every other dial position.

This produced the three numbers, but did not give the order in which they occurred. The final stage was to try the different combinations of the numbers, and shouldn't take very long – if the numbers chosen were correct there would only be six possibilities for the sequence.

If that didn't work, it would be necessary to go either side of the numbers obtained, so if the first number was believed to be four, then three and five would have to be tried. For a three-number lock, this would mean a hundred and sixty-two possibilities, and up to that number of attempts would have to be tried. Had there been four numbers, it would have meant nearly two thousand possible combinations, and could hardly have been completed before daylight, unless luck was very much on his side. Indeed, if the safe had been equipped with more than three numbers in the combination, he would probably have abandoned the enterprise immediately.

DEATH OF A SAFEBREAKER

As it was, he proceeded with the laborious task of listening to the clicks through his stethoscope as he turned the dial first one way, then the other. Every few seconds, he made a mark on his graph.

There were no extraneous noises. No passing vehicles, or the rumble of underground trains, or the sound of footsteps on pavements, for example, one or more of which occurred during most of his other safe-breaking exploits. So he progressed smoothly enough, and was confident about the three numbers his chart eventually produced – 5; 29; 61.

It had taken him almost an hour to complete this stage. He stood up and stretched, but then knelt down again without turning around.

The next phase didn't take very long. If he was spot on with his figures, there were now only six possibilities. He only needed three attempts – the combination was 29; 5; 61.

He swung the heavy door open, and shone his head lamp inside.

A quiet artificial throat-clearing noise from behind him made him jump to his feet and turn.

The watcher had risen silently and moved to within ten feet of the man. As the burglar turned away from the safe, the watcher switched on a torch, and without speaking immediately fired two shots from a silenced automatic pistol. The man slumped to the floor without uttering a sound.

The killer knew that in this house even the interior walls were very thick, and the oak door likewise almost soundproof. The term 'silencer' was misleading – the suppressor only reduced the sound of the shot. Nevertheless, it was unlikely that anything would have been heard – even if a listener had been just outside the door.

The killer placed the gun on the floor beside the body, and – still wearing gloves – reached into the safe. Ignoring two bundles of banknotes and a small cashbox, the murderer pulled out a cardboard box. First the lid was removed, and then some documents. After a swift riffle through these, a number of the papers were selected and placed on the floor by the safebreaker's notepad. The box was returned to the safe, the money still untouched.

The safe door was closed, the lightbulbs were quickly replaced, and the chair returned to its usual position.

Almost as an afterthought, and without any conscious reasoning, the gun was pushed underneath the body.

The killer then took the papers purloined from the safe, and the safecracker's notepad, and with one last glance around the room left via the internal door.

In the hallway, still using only intermittent torchlight, the killer went through to the scullery and thence via some stairs down to the boiler room. Here, a coke furnace was still functioning.

Carefully opening the fire door, the gloves, documents, and the safebreaker's notepad were all fed in. Knowing that no sound from here would ever penetrate to the rest of the house, the killer put a shovelful of coke on top of the items already consigned to the fire – which had sprung to life as the paper touched the still-hot coke.

After watching the conflagration for some time, the fire door was closed again. The killer returned to the main part of the house, and after listening carefully at the bottom of the stairs, returned to bed. Or rather, went to bed for the first time that night.

CHAPTER 2

The great house in which the killing had occurred had, until a few years before, been in the same family for almost two hundred years. But in 1933, the last squire died without issue. The distant relative who inherited had neither the means nor the desire to occupy the property, and promptly put the estate up for sale.

The new owner, although titled, was not of ancient aristocratic lineage. Some might have described him as *nouveau riche*, but if that implied some untravelled and poorly-educated former peasant then the description would have been most unfair.

Edgar Tallis was solidly middle class, the son of a doctor. Educated at a minor public school, he had gone on to read physics and engineering at Manchester, before starting up in business himself. His mother, the only daughter of a Lancashire mill owner, had been able and willing to provide substantial capital. Over the next ten years, his businesses prospered.

By 1912, he had spotted two things. First, that a major war appeared inevitable, and would arrive sooner or later. Second, that factories supplying Government needs would require machinery to an unprecedented extent. His companies already provided all sorts of such equipment. Some of his machinery was being used in the manufacture of vehicles with external combustion engines – railway locomotives, traction engines, and ships. Increasingly, some was used for making vehicles using internal combustion engines – motor cars, lorries, and more recently aeroplanes. He started gearing up to increase his output.

By 1914, Tallis, already wealthy, was a crucial player in the preparations for war. During the next few years, he became even richer, although it would have been very unfair to call him a profiteer.

Indeed, the Government recognised his contribution to the nation, and three years into the war he was awarded a knighthood. Then in 1919, he was raised to the peerage by Lloyd George's Coalition Government, becoming the first Baron Tallis of Newenden in the County of Kent – taking his new title from the village in which he had been born.

In 1934, the National Government under the Labour Prime Minister Ramsay MacDonald recognised his continuing work as being significantly beneficial for the country. Tallis was pushed one rung further up the peerage ladder. He now became the first Viscount Tallis of Wythall in the County of Worcestershire, after the house and estate not far outside Birmingham which he had purchased the year before.

***

As part of the purchase arrangements for the estate, Tallis had agreed – indeed had requested – that any of the existing staff who wished to continue in their positions should transfer to him. Although many had reservations initially, almost all of those concerned decided to stay on. This was, of course, in the depths of the Great Depression, and other jobs were not exactly numerous.

Within a week of completing the purchase, Tallis arranged meetings with what might be called the 'heads of department' in his new little empire.

The Land Agent, the Butler, the Head Gardener, and the Housekeeper were all called in, one at a time. Each interview lasted about an hour, and each of the four left the room substantially happier than when they had entered it. An unasked-for pay rise awarded to them helped, certainly, but it was the general attitude of their new employer which counted most. Two examples will suffice.

That evening, Orson Deedes, the Agent, reported the conversation to his wife. "He said to me, 'I know nothing about estate management. I've made extensive enquiries about you, and heard nothing but good. So, I'm giving you more-or-less a free hand. Give me a written report once a month – nothing lengthy. Come and see me any time I'm here. If you want to spend a significant amounts of money – say over five hundred pounds, make an outline case in writing and then come and persuade me face to face. I do shoot, by the way, but don't have much time. We need to discuss whether to offer some of the shooting rights to a syndicate, but there's no hurry.'

"He seems a very decent chap, and I liked him. Of course, he didn't get where he is today by being a fool. By the way, you and I will be invited to lunch and dine with the family from time to time."

Herbert Partridge, the Butler, was similarly impressed. Without a wife with whom to discuss the matter, he spoke to the Cook, while the kitchen was temporarily free of maids and footmen.

"Well, Mrs Green, I'll admit to being relieved. First off, he's assured me that he has no intention of rushing in and changing the old routines on the first day. He's going to 'play it by ear', he says, but he doesn't expect to alter much of anything.

"I knew nothing about him, but he seems to be just as much a gentleman as our last master, God rest him. Certainly he'll know how to use the cutlery!"

The Housekeeper and the Head Gardener, had they been asked, would have given similar reports. And after a few months, even the two most junior members of the household staff, the scullery maid and the boot boy, were as content as someone in their lowly positions could hope to be.

In short, as far as the employees went,

everyone was happy.

**

Up to a point, Tallis's family was also content. Lady Tallis had died during the Spanish Flu pandemic in 1919, only weeks after her husband took his seat in the House of Lords.

His remaining immediate family members were his son and his three daughters. Of all these, Tallis was very fond. He also approved of his daughter-in-law and one son-in-law. He had never been particularly enamoured of the other two sons-in-law, and he had a strong dislike of several of their friends.

He had reasons – very good reasons – for his views.

Tallis, with enormous wealth, a seat in the House of Lords, and contacts with numerous people in various high places, was in a position to acquire information about anyone he wanted, whether that might be a fellow peer or a felon.

And, conscious that his four children were not only comfortably off – each had a generous allowance and also held directorships in his companies – but would one day be even richer, for some years he had taken it upon himself to 'vet' friends – and especially would-be partners. Although a tough no-nonsense businessman, he was essentially an honest straightforward man, and this checking up was probably the only less-than-honourable thing he ever did. He didn't look on it as being anything of the kind, of course, and in the circumstances perhaps many other people would agree with him.

The four offspring were largely unaware of their father's investigations. He had, for example, never made the slightest attempt to frighten off the two sons-in-law of whom he disapproved. Nor, indeed, had he tried to dissuade either of the two girls from their marriages, although had his wife remained alive it is likely that she, knowing what her husband suspected (and later knew), would not have remained silent.

However, four people present in the house were aware that he held information about them – and all were worried. None knew of the others' concerns.

CHAPTER 3

On the morning after the murder, the first movements came from various servants. One, who had various duties including cleaning boots, came down to the boiler room, and replenished the boiler fire. He noticed nothing unusual, and simply piled on more fuel, before starting the unpleasant task of 'riddling' the firebox and removing ash. The Cook started to prepare breakfast, and a maid began the process of making tea. Trays – for those who liked early morning tea in bed – had been made ready the previous evening. Nobody currently in residence took their breakfast in bed.

On the other side of the baize door, a parlourmaid moved from room to room, opening curtains ready for the new day.

Tallis himself was away in the United States, on business, but all four of his children were currently in residence, together with their partners and a sprinkling of friends. All his grandchildren were elsewhere – being cared for either by nannies or different grandparents. The reason for the gathering – only the eldest daughter and her husband lived permanently in the great house – was the forthcoming fortieth birthday of the son and heir. His father had sent sincere apologies for missing the occasion, but, as the family knew, he was in America at the behest of the Government.

In the breakfast room, a footman and another maid were engaged in stocking the sideboard with the various items expected at a gentleman's table. (The Butler rarely involved himself at breakfast when the Master was away from the house, unless – a rare occurrence in his absence – a very important guest was in residence.

The arrival of the first three occupants in the breakfast room, coincided with the arrival of a maid in the study.

Tallis's son and heir, the Honourable Walter Tallis, had just sat down at the table. His sister Patricia was at the sideboard, with Cissie Saunders, the guest of another sister, beside her.

The breakfast room door was open, as Agnes, another parlourmaid, was just bringing in another dish.

A shrill scream was heard by everyone in the room – Agnes very nearly dropped her plate.

Tallis put down the knife and fork which he had only just picked up. Had the Butler or even one of the footmen been present, he would have despatched him to see what the noise was about. Feeling that perhaps sending one of the maids might be inappropriate, he rose himself. "I'd better go and see what that's about," he muttered, and left the room.

Patricia, a matronly blonde with a pleasant face, a few years older than her brother, looked at Cissie and shrugged. "One of the maids has seen a mouse or a spider, perhaps," she suggested.

Cissie, perhaps fifteen years younger, and shorter and darker, allowed her thin lips to move into a smile. "Probably," she agreed. The two women took their plates to the table and sat down, several places apart. The maid busied herself with pouring coffee.

Once outside the room Tallis could see, some sixty feet along the hallway, one of the maids sitting on a chair, sobbing. He moved rapidly towards her. Simultaneously the Housekeeper, Mrs Hobbs, and a footman, Pettit, came through the door from the kitchen, evidently having heard the scream too. All three arrived at the crying girl at the same time.

"What on earth is it, Lizzie?" enquired Mrs Hobbs. Poor Lizzie could hardly speak coherently, but the listeners managed to grasp that there was a dead man in the Master's study.

Tallis moved swiftly the few yards to the study. The door was open, as the maid had evidently left it when fleeing. He stopped on the threshold, and looked in. The door was in the middle of one wall, and looking to his right he saw nothing unusual. The half-open door obstructed his view to the left. Gently pushing the door even wider so he could see past it, he immediately saw what Lizzie had seen.

He paused for a moment, then turned to the Housekeeper, who with the footman had followed him to the door. "Please go and call Doctor Bailey, Mrs Hobbs. Pettit, go and find Mr Partridge. Present my compliments, and ask him to come down here as soon as possible."

He then returned to the still-sobbing maid. "Nasty shock for you, Lizzie. I can't see who it is from the doorway – did you recognise him?"

The girl shook her head. "No, sir – but I didn't really stop to look."

"No, of course not. Well, run along now to the breakfast room, and ask Mrs Burgess to come to the study. Don't say why. Then go straight to the kitchen, and tell Cook I've said you're to have a glass of brandy and a cup of strong tea or coffee. Then just sit down and do nothing. Understand?"

The girl nodded, gave her nose and eyes a final mopping, and went off.

Tallis returned to the study, this time going in. He moved a little closer to the body, which was lying face down. He immediately realised that, whoever it was, it was not a house guest. The dead man was dressed in a poor-quality jacket and trousers. The underside of the shoes showed signs of wear, such that one wouldn't want to wear them anywhere near a puddle – although they did show signs of mud.

Lizzie had switched on the lights on entering the room, but had not got as far as opening the heavy curtains. Tallis now went to the windows, and started to draw the curtains back. He was on the second curtain when he saw the circular hole in the glass. He paused and was looking at this, thinking of the implication, when his sister arrived in the doorway.

"What's the fuss, Walter? I assume it was Lizzie screaming, but she just told me to come here and then shot off still snivelling."

Without speaking, Tallis pointed across the room, and Patricia turned in that direction.

"Oh God!" she exclaimed, immediately seeing the body. "Who is it?"

"No idea, Sis. But the French window is damaged, and he obviously got in from outside. The stethoscope beside him suggests a safebreaker rather than a doctor, I fancy. The safe's intact, though, and as he's still here clearly he hasn't got away with anything."

"A heart attack, do you think?"

"I suppose so. I told Mrs Hobbs to call Doctor Bailey, if she can get hold of him. But I suppose we'd better call the police as well."

As he spoke, the Butler arrived at the study door, with the Housekeeper a pace behind.

"You sent for me, sir? Mrs Hobbs has acquainted me with the position here," said Partridge.

"And I've spoken to Dr Bailey, sir," interjected the Housekeeper. "He'll come along directly."

"Good. Right. Mrs Burgess and I don't

recognise the dead man, but he is clearly a burglar – broke the glass to get access through the French doors, it seems. So I'm going to call the police.

"Meantime, Partridge, you stay outside this door. Nobody is to be allowed into this room. Mrs Hobbs, you go back and tell all the staff to carry on as normal. You'll have to say what's happened, of course – although I expect Lizzie has already done that!"

When the two members of staff had gone, Tallis suggested that his sister should return to the breakfast room, and inform people about the incident as they came down.

Trying to ignore the nearby body, Tallis went to his father's desk, and sat down, drawing the telephone nearer.

He was pleased to learn from the operator that the village bobby had been connected to the telephone network recently, and she put him through. When Tallis explained who he was, and what he wished to report, Constable Pardoe hesitated. "I'll come up to the hall right away, sir, but from what you say this'll likely be needing detectives and so on. I'll get on the station before I come."

Replacing the handset, Tallis left the room, enjoined Partridge to remain at his post, and returned to his breakfast. In his absence, all the other guests had come downstairs. Patricia had of course explained the finding of the body, but after the initial chatter everyone seemed to lose interest

– there were, after all, no useful facts on which to base a discussion. The conversations around the breakfast table were therefore more-or-less on traditional topics. Tallis signalled to a maid to remove his cold food, and went back for a fresh plate at the sideboard.

None of the fourteen people present seemed to be put off their food in any way.

To the footman, Tallis gave a further instruction. "Mr Partridge is guarding the study, Pettit. So listen for the doorbell, and when it rings, you go and answer it. It may be the doctor, or the police – although I suppose Constable Pardoe might go to the kitchen door. Show whoever it is into the study.

Tallis looked across the table at his eldest sister. "Apologies, Pat – you're the chatelaine here, of course. Do you want to take charge, as it were?"

Patricia smiled. "Oh no, Walt, thanks. Carry on. You're the heir, and anyway I think dealing with a burglar is man's work!"

CHAPTER 4

Some twenty minutes later, ten of the original fourteen people at breakfast still remained, drinking last cups of tea or coffee and having a general chat. Pettit returned.

He coughed gently to announce his presence, and the talk died away.

Unsure whether to address the notional chatelaine or the heir, the man attempted to include both – a difficult task as they were seated on opposite sides of the table.

"Doctor Bailey has arrived, as has Constable Pardoe, sir, madam. Er…the doctor had hardly got inside the study when he said the man was shot. They ask if you would go to the study at once, sir."

For a few seconds silence reigned, then several people started talking simultaneously. Tallis got up, and moved quickly to the door. Over his shoulder as he left the room he asked that nobody should go anywhere near the study.

Arriving at the study a few seconds later, he found Pardoe, Bailey and Partridge standing together by the door.

The doctor, who had been ministering to the occupants of the hall in the previous squire's time, had met Tallis on a number of occasions.

"Bad business," he said. "The man's been shot. I gather you don't know him?"

"Shot? Oh God. Well, I haven't seen the face, but from his clothing he's not a guest, nor a member of the staff here. And since he seems to have broken in, I assume he's a burglar."

"We've got him turned over now, sir," said Pardoe. "Would you mind just taking a look, sir? You too, Mr Partridge."

Walter and the Butler reluctantly stepped into the study and approached the body. They saw a man in his fifties, with thin and greying hair and a ferrety-looking face. Each man took a quick look and immediately shook his head.

"Well," said the Doctor, "Pardoe tells me that the CID people are coming. The body will have to stay where it is for the moment. There'll have to be a *post mortem*, of course, and an inquest in due course."

"Will you be doing the autopsy?" asked Tallis.

"Not my province. The police have their own man. But I can tell you now exactly what he'll say. This man was shot twice. At least one bullet – probably both – entered his heart, and so he died. Somewhere between midnight and two o'clock, I estimate.

"Incidentally, the gun, which is a silenced automatic" – he pointed to the nearby desk, on which the pistol was now lying – "was found beneath the body. He wasn't shot at point blank range – there's no powder marks or anything, but obviously from not more than about twenty feet away as the room isn't very long. So no question of suicide, I'm afraid, Tallis.

"I've informed the Coroner and the Police Surgeon, by telephone. Nothing more that I can do, so I'll be off – although perhaps I should wait to see the investigating officer first."

"Come and have a cup of coffee, Doc, while you're waiting. Assuming Pardoe is going to guard the room, you can carry on now, Partridge."

Tallis led the Doctor to the breakfast room, where six people were still present – all three of Walter's siblings, two of their spouses, and his own wife. None of the visiting friends remained in the room. As everyone had met the Doctor before, no introductions were necessary. The Doctor declined the offer of something to eat, but accepted a cup of coffee from the maid still standing by the buffet.

Tallis took a fresh cup of coffee too, and after dismissing the maid gave those present a summary of the situation.

Everyone sat in silence for a minute.

His wife Jill spoke first. "You say this can't be suicide. So I suppose two of them arrived and then he had a falling-out with his partner in crime."

There was another silence, as everyone digested her hypothesis.

"Possible, certainly, and let's hope you're right, Jill," said Cornelius Burgess, Pat's husband. "Seems a bit odd, though. Burglars in this country don't generally carry guns, or so I've heard. And why shoot his colleague here anyway? No – I think we'd better brace ourselves for different enquiries."

"What do you mean, Cornelius?" asked Emily, the youngest sibling.

"Just this, Em. Unless it is well known that this man always worked with someone else, the police are almost certain to think he was shot by someone in the house."

"Oh God!" exclaimed Patricia and Charity in unison.

"But why?" asked Craig Starling, Emily's husband. "If someone heard the burglar, armed himself, and went down and shot the man, surely he would simply tell everyone? Not something to be too ashamed about."

"I don't think Cornelius has that scenario in mind," replied Tallis, "and it doesn't seem a very likely one anyway. If someone heard what they thought was a burglar, I think they'd raise the alarm. No – there's not much doubt that this man was killed by his 'partner in crime' – but I'm afraid that was probably someone from inside the house. Someone who knew the burglar was coming. If that is the case, then a member of staff is most likely, of course – but that won't stop the police asking us a lot of intrusive questions."

There was another silence.

"Not my job to act as detective," remarked the Doctor, joining in for the first time, "but does anyone in the house possess a pistol?"

There was a general shaking of heads. "There are several shotguns in the house," said Walter, "and those of us who live elsewhere all have shotguns too. But I'm pretty sure Father doesn't have any other firearms in the house, and I've never heard that any of the rest of us do." He looked around the table, where every head was shaking.

Charity, the only sibling whose spouse wasn't in the room, confirmed that Norman didn't own any weapon – again other than a couple of shotguns.

Nobody said anything about the six non-family guests, but everyone except the Doctor (who didn't know that anyone else was visiting) was mentally considering them. Those thoughts proving inconclusive, the family moved on to review the members of staff.

In this lull, a maid tapped at the door and announced that two detectives had arrived.

"You'll want time to speak to them first, Doc; I'll come along in a few minutes," suggested Tallis.

Bailey left with the maid, and Tallis sighed. "Rather spoiled the celebrations," he remarked. "But as Father couldn't be here anyway, perhaps we'd better abandon the whole thing and re-schedule it for when he can be present."

His relations all nodded in agreement.

"Where is everyone else?" he enquired.

His wife shrugged. "Everyone agreed it was too horrible outside to go for a walk. Cora, Cissie,

Eustace and Jonathan all said they had letters to write. Bruce said it was a bit early in the day, but invited Maurice to the billiards room for a smoke and a game."

Patricia stood up. I think I'd better go and get the servants together and explain what we know so far. I'll not mention our speculations, naturally.

"Good," said Tallis. "Well, I'd better go and see the police. I assume you'll agree to them basing themselves in the study, Sis?"

Patricia nodded. "I for one won't want to go in there again for a long time."

"Nor will I," added Charity, "and I haven't even been in to see the body!"

CHAPTER 5

Returning to the study, Tallis found Constable Pardoe standing outside the open door. Tapping on it, Pardoe announced, "Mr Tallis is here, sir."

Someone called "come in," and the Constable stood aside to allow Walter to go in. He found Dr Bailey standing by the damaged window, talking to a short tubby man in a rumpled dark suit. Another man, also in plain clothes, was crouching by the body, apparently engaged in taking photographs.

Bailey introduced the tubby man. This is Inspector Rees, Tallis, and over there is Sergeant Knowles. Knowles raised an arm in acknowledgement, and Tallis extended his hand to the Inspector.

The two men looked at each other. Rees was just on the wrong side of fifty, with pepper-and-salt hair and horn-rimmed spectacles.

"I'll gather my bits and get off now, gentlemen – you know where I am if you want me," announced Bailey.

"Well, Mr Tallis, this is a rum do and no mistake," began the Inspector, speaking in a Worcestershire accent. "Let's sit down. I understand you don't recognise the deceased?"

"That's right, Inspector. Neither I nor Partridge – he's the Butler – have ever seen the man before."

"No. Well, sir, our first job is to identify him. His pockets are empty except for a key – ignition key almost certainly. We're checking his prints, but that'll take time. Then we need to find out how he got here – car is likely, but we don't know for sure. You saw the stethoscope, no doubt. Doesn't look like a medical man" – here the doctor snorted as he was leaving the room – "so we may surmise that he is what is known as a cracksman. One of the tools of the trade, is a stethoscope. So it's pretty clear he came for the safe.

"Now, sir, let me just explain my current thinking. We've looked at the footmarks just inside these doors where he evidently came in. On the wooden floor before the carpet starts there is only the one set of footmarks – it's pretty muddy outside, of course. Also, your Butler confirms that before I arrived all the external doors were still locked and bolted.

"This wasn't a falling out among thieves. No. An inside job, I'm afraid."

Tallis looked at him, and managed a faint smile. "Some of the family members were having a discussion a few minutes ago, and we came to much the same conclusion."

"Well, of course that's not definite, as yet." The Inspector fell silent, and waited.

Tallis thought for a moment. "My father is

away in America at present," he said. "My three sisters and I are here at present. Our spouses are here too, but not our children. We're here for a birthday celebration – for my birthday, actually. There are six other guests, friends of one sort or another. My eldest sister Patricia is really in charge – our Mother is long dead. Pat effectively keeps house for Father, and she and her husband live here. So I'll need to talk to her, Inspector. I can't think what you might want to look for, but I imagine she would give her consent for your men to search the place – save you the trouble of obtaining a warrant."

"Thank you sir; very helpful that might be, although as you say at present we have nothing specific to look for. Now, would you be able to let me have a list of everyone in the house at present – family, visitors, servants?"

"Yes, certainly. Again, I'll need to discuss that with Pat – I don't know the full names of several members of staff. Let me go and talk to her now, and I'll come back inside ten minutes with the list."

"Just one other thing, sir. Did any of the visitors – family or guests – bring their own servants?"

"No, Inspector, as it happened nobody did."

***

Tallis went in search of Patricia, and eventually found her in the servants' hall, talking to most if not all of the inside staff. He waited for her to finish, and then walked back with her. Passing the open door of the drawing room, they could hear that several people were inside, so he guided his sister into a small room known as the writing room.

"This'll do, Sis," he remarked. "The police want a list of everyone here. You know all the staff, of course, so will you do that, please?"

Patricia nodded, took a sheet of paper from the rack on the writing desk, and started to scribble. The task took only five minutes, and while she was doing that he jotted down the names of the eight family members and the six guests.

After looking over what she had written, she pushed her paper over to her brother.

She looked at him, realising that he had something more to say.

"It seems the Inspector is thinking on the lines I outlined earlier, Sis. Someone from inside the house."

Patricia nodded slowly. "Oh lord, what a mess."

"One other thing. I said that you probably wouldn't object if he wants to search the house, although for the moment he doesn't need to do that."

"Fair enough," replied Pat, who seemed to be thinking of something else.

"Look, Walt. It goes without saying that

none of the family would do this. I see no reason for any of the staff to do it either. I fear that we'll have to think about the guests."

Tallis nodded. "Yes, although I'm pretty sure the police won't simply rule out family members like you have! But, it has to be said, the guests are a pretty odd mix. It couldn't even be said that each of us siblings is particularly enamoured of every one of the six. Nor are our respective partners, come to that. Basically each guest is a friend of only one – or of one pair – of the eight of us.

"I'm not keen on Charity's friend Bruce, for a start, and I'm pretty sure you would never have invited Cissie yourself."

Patricia didn't demur.

"Going back to what we discussed earlier – abandoning the party. I'd do that like a shot – not being funny – and get rid of the guests, but I rather think the police won't allow anyone to leave yet.

Tallis shook his head, and rose to take both lists to the Inspector.

***

In the study, he found Inspector Rees on the telephone. He turned to go out again, but the DI, keeping the receiver to his ear, waved the main part of the telephone to indicate that Tallis should come in.

Tallis guessed from the half of the conversation he could hear that Rees was talking to the Coroner. A few minutes later, the Inspector hung up the receiver, and sat down in the armchair opposite the one which Tallis had chosen. Neither of them would ever be aware of this, but the DI was sitting in the same chair that the murderer had used earlier while waiting.

"Well, sir, I've spoken to my Superintendent. It seems the Chief Constable thinks us locals should be able to sort this one without going to the Yard for help. All very well," he added morosely, "but we don't have the experience. In forty years, I've only seen one murder around here, and that was fifteen years ago. Quite obvious who did that one anyway – no detective work involved. I retire in a few months, and I can see my last case being a failure."

He shook his head. "Sorry, sir, please forget I said any of that – I shouldn't have spoken out loud. Anyway, that was the Coroner on the telephone when you came in. I've explained that we don't even know who the dead man is yet, so Mr Smallbone won't open the inquest for a couple of days.

"Anyway, as I said before, our first task is to identify the man. I've sent my Sergeant off to London. He has taken the dead man's fingerprints, and a roll of film with pictures of the man's face which will be developed when he gets there. I'm hoping the Yard'll have a record of the man."

"You don't think he's a local criminal then, Inspector?"

"Not from within the county, sir, no. I've

never come across a professional safebreaker here – and there can't be a large supply of targets anyway. He could of course be from Birmingham, and certainly my money is on him being either a Londoner or a Brummie. Plenty of safes in cities – one in almost every office, probably, although not all combination ones, I suppose. If he's not known at the Yard, I'll try Birmingham. But I think London has more specialists of this sort, so I'm trying there first.

"Now, I have no experience of guns. But Doctor Bailey served in the War, and he tells me something which seems highly significant. The pistol is…" he paused to consult his notebook… "a Webley self-loading pistol, calibre 0.32. Very common, apparently, both in this and a larger calibre. But the Doc says he has never seen one like this. Someone seems to have adapted it to allow a suppressor – that's a silencer to you and me – to be fitted to the barrel. Presumably screwed on. That's been done by a skilled mechanic – a weapons expert, it would seem. A crooked gunsmith, even. Furthermore, the serial numbers have been ground off. No chance of tracing the source.

"What you're saying, Inspector, is that this pistol was deliberately altered by – or at least on behalf of – a professional criminal. Presumably to be used as here – to kill fairly silently."

"Exactly, sir. And it's one reason why I guess a London man is more probable than a Brummie one.

"Now, you have that list for me?"

Tallis handed over the two lists. He'd glanced over Patricia's while walking along the corridor, and noted that she had supplied the job title for each servant, as well as the name.

Rees quickly scanned both lists, and then put them down on the little table beside his armchair. He looked at Tallis.

"Well, sir, we seem to have three separate sets of suspects. There's no easy way of saying this, but one group is the family – you, your sisters, and your respective partners. Then there are these six guests – four men and two women, I see. And finally, there are the staff. I assume, by the way, that this list only includes those who sleep in the house – not gardeners and the like?"

"That's correct, Inspector. The outside staff don't sleep in, nor do they have keys to the back door. And I can't object to your including the family in the list of suspects – even though I refuse to believe any of us is a murderer."

Rees grunted.

"Now, a couple of questions arise," he said. "What was there of value in the safe? And, following on from that – if as I suspect the burglar came from 'the smoke', why did he come here?"

There was silence for a full minute. Then, without addressing the questions, Tallis spoke again.

"Actually, Inspector, there's something else which seems very curious to me. All the ground floor windows were heavily curtained last night, as you'd expect. Nobody could see from outside which was the drawing room, dining room, breakfast room, writing room, library study, or whatever. Yet, assuming you've not found any other places where he tried to gain access, this man went straight to the window of the room with the safe. How did he know?"

"That's quite right, sir. You'll agree that makes an inside accomplice almost certain."

There was another silence. Tallis spoke again. "But it doesn't make sense. If this was a sort of joint venture, why should one then kill the other?"

"I can't answer that, yet. But going back to my earlier question – what was there of value in the safe?"

"I really have no idea. Father has only lived here for about four years, and I've never actually seen the safe open. After my Mother died, about eighteen years ago, I remember him saying that he would keep her jewellery in the safe at our old house, and not put it in the bank. But over the years I think he has given most of the pieces away – to my sisters and to my wife. I don't know what, if anything, remains, but it's possible there is something. It's also possible there might be papers in there relating to his business – and of course some of that concerns confidential Government contracts. But I should have thought most of that stuff would be in his office. Sorry, Inspector, but I can't help there."

"Who else might know the combination, sir?"

"I doubt if anyone does. As I said, Patricia lives here, but I'd bet any money that she doesn't know it. Father has a male secretary who is also something of a confidant. His name is Meredith Hammond, and on the rare occasions that Father has a business meeting in the house, Hammond is always in attendance and stays over. For example, from time to time we have a board meeting here – we hold them in the dining room, actually.

"Hammond is a very remarkable man – qualified both as a solicitor and as an accountant. But even though he has my father's absolute trust, I doubt if even he has access to this safe."

"You're on the board, are you sir?"

"There are five companies, Inspector. Yes, I'm a director of each one. My wife and my sisters are all directors of at least one of the companies. One of my brothers-in-law, Pat's husband Cornelius Burgess, also has two directorships. Of the immediate family, only Norman Carey, married to my sister Charity, and Craig Starling, Emily's husband, are not directly involved in any of the businesses."

"I see; thank you. You said Lord Tallis is in America – when did he go?"

"He sailed on the *Ile de France* the day before yesterday – it docks in New York sometime tomorrow or the day after, I think. I suppose we could send a wireless message to the ship to ask him about the contents, and who might know the combination."

"Hmm. When does he come back to England?"

"He has a passage provisionally booked on the *Normandie* in a fortnight or so. But he really wants to try the *Queen Mary*, and I think he might look for an excuse to delay his return so he could time his return to tie in with her sailing.

"He's not actually staying in New York – he takes a train to Washington DC as soon as he docks. I'm not sure where he is staying in Washington, but no doubt Hammond will know."

"I see." Rees drummed his fingers on the side table. "I'll think about using the wireless. In the meantime, I'd like you to do two things. First, please ask your sister – Mrs Burgess, is it? – if she does know the combination. Second, I'd be grateful if you will organise a roster for me to interview the family and guests. Fifteen minutes for each will be ample, I think. After that – and it'll probably be tomorrow – I'll see the staff.

"I don't want to ask anyone else – especially not the ladies – to come in here with the body still lying on the floor, but it'll be removed in the next half hour, so perhaps we could start at twelve noon?

"Oh, and I want to talk to this Hammond chap – do you have a contact number for him?"

"Father's address book is in the centre

drawer of the desk, Inspector." Tallis rose and retrieved it. "Yes, it's here – numbers for both the office and his home." He handed the book to Rees, and moved towards the door.

"I'll have your first candidate here at twelve."

CHAPTER 6

Rees got up from his armchair with an audible sigh, and went to sit at the desk. He called to Constable Pardoe, who was still standing outside the study door.

"Right, Pardoe. Go to the kitchen and see if they can give you a small box or something. We'll put the gun in it, and you can take it back to the station and get someone to dust it for fingerprints. Waste of time, but it'll have to be done. Off you go."

The Inspector reached for the telephone, and gave the office number listed against Hammond's name. It took several minutes for the connection to be made, and several more after that before – after threatening to charge a difficult subordinate with obstruction of a police officer – he was finally put through to the man he wanted.

"What can I do for you, Inspector?" asked Hammond, when Rees had identified himself.

The Inspector explained the situation at the Tallis house. Hammond let out a whistle after only two sentences.

"Great Scott!" he exclaimed, when Rees had finished, "I don't think his lordship is going to be pleased! You know he is on his way to the States, I assume?"

"Yes – Mr Tallis has been explaining that. I need to know two things. First – do you know the combination for the safe, and second, do you know what items of value there might be inside it?"

"I have no idea about the combination, Inspector. Nor do I know what might be inside. All I'd say is that it's unlikely there would be any confidential business papers in it – everything like that is in another safe here in the office. I do know how to get into this one.

"I imagine, although I'm not certain, that when there is a board meeting in the house, Lord Tallis probably puts papers in the house safe, before returning them to the office afterwards. However, it's a month since the last meeting there, and there isn't another scheduled for another three weeks, so as I say it seems unlikely that there are any commercial papers inside. Private papers, possibly."

"Right – thank you Mr Hammond. As we don't know as yet what the man was after, and it's still possible that's what he was seeking, you might think it wise to put some sort of guard on your office safe for a while."

"I see that, yes. I'll put that in hand. Lord Tallis always expects to be kept abreast of anything happening, and although I was going to wait until he reached Washington before contacting him, I think I'd better try to send him a Marconigram or whatever they're called these days."

"I intend to do the same thing, Mr

Hammond, but you go ahead anyway.

"Oh, help me on one other thing. What are the relative positions of Lord Tallis and his son – and the other family members – on these boards?"

"There are five companies, Inspector. Lord Tallis is executive chairman of three, and chairman of the other two. Walter is managing director of those two, and an ordinary director of the first three.

"Mr Burgess, Walter's brother-in-law, is the finance director of two companies – he's an accountant by profession. Walter's wife and his three sisters also hold various non-executive directorships.

"These are all privately owned companies, of course. Almost all of the shares are held by the family. A handful – around 5% across the companies – are held by outsiders. I have a small number myself, in fact, gifted to me only a few months ago. I used to be the company secretary for one of the firms, but Lord Tallis offered me a very decent salary to work for him across all five, so I resigned my original role. I'm now employed by him personally, not by any of the companies."

"I'm going to read you a list of six names, Mr Hammond, and I'd like you to tell me if you've heard of any of them, and if any have a connection with one of the Tallis companies." He read out the six names from the list of guests in front of him.

Hammond hesitated. "I've heard of all six, certainly," he replied slowly. "I can tell you that none is a director or an employee of a Tallis company. I'm in some difficulty, Inspector. However, I suppose this is a murder enquiry. All I can say is that I've had the job of, shall we say, looking into some of those people. Further than that I can't go. You'll need to ask Lord Tallis for any further information."

"I see," said Rees. He thought for a moment. "This 'looking into' people – have you had to do that for anyone other than some of those in the house?"

"Yes, occasionally. But I really can't go into any more detail. You'll need to convince me – and probably Lord Tallis – that this line of questioning is definitely relevant to your enquiry."

"Well, I won't press you on this for now, Mr Hammond. But all the people presently in the house are suspects. It is quite clear that anything about them is relevant to my enquiry. Especially if there is any information which might suggest criminality."

Hammond didn't comment on that, and shortly after the call was ended.

Pardoe had returned during the conversation, and was standing by the desk with two small green and white boxes.

"Best I could do, sir," said the constable. "I thought if the silencer thing came off and went in one box, the gun might go in the other."

"Good thinking, Pardoe," said Rees, smiling for the first time since he had arrived in the house.

"I bet this'll be the first time one of Mr Kellogg's cereal boxes has been used for holding a pistol!" He measured the boxes by eye. "Yes, reckon you're right."

Taking out his handkerchief, and touching the gun as sparingly as possible, he carefully unscrewed the silencer. Then, using a pen he eased the pistol into one box and the silencer into the other.

"Now see here, Pardoe, the pistol is still loaded and dangerous. The safety catch thing is on, but accidents can still happen. Get this back to the station.

"I assume you came here on your bicycle. Can you drive?"

"Yes, sir."

Good. Take my car to go back to the station. See Superintendent Foster. I have nobody left in CID until Knowles gets back from London – one of our DCs is away and the other is sick. So ask if the Super can find someone experienced in small arms who can dust the pistol for prints. Give them the warning I've just given you. When the surface has been checked for prints, tell them to check on the magazine surface too. After that, it should be locked away. Got that?"

"Yes, sir, got all that."

"Right, next job. Take these names, and ask the Super if he can get someone to go through our records, and see if anything is known against any of these people. Failing that, we need to try

Scotland Yard's records."

Rees rapidly wrote the names of family members and guests on a separate sheet, and handed the new list to Pardoe. He did not include the members of staff. He also passed over his car ignition key.

"When you've seen to that, bring the car back and then resume your normal duties."

Pardoe confirmed that he understood what the DI wanted, and left the room carrying the two boxes somewhat gingerly in front of his chest.

As he went out, a maid arrived at the door, escorting two ambulance men carrying a stretcher. She quickly scurried away, avoiding looking into the room at all.

"Come in, lads," instructed Rees. He gestured to the body. "He's all yours. Get him to the morgue. Doctor Gifford will do the *post mortem* this afternoon."

After the body had been removed, it was clear that there were some bloodstains on the carpet. The DI was just contemplating these when there was a tap on the door and Walter Tallis put his head into the study.

"Come in, Mr Tallis," said Rees.

"I've got Patricia with me," said the man. "As I thought, she doesn't know the combination. But as she's already seen the body she volunteered to come and be interviewed first even if it was still here – but I see it's gone anyway."

He introduced his sister to the DI.

"While I talk to Mrs Burgess, I wonder if you could find something to cover the blood stains, Mr Tallis. A blanket, or a big towel, perhaps – but not a white one."

Tallis nodded in understanding, and left again.

"Perhaps we could just sit down over there, madam," suggested Rees, and the two moved across the room to the armchairs.

"Now, I understand that you don't know the combination numbers for the safe, but do you have any idea of what is inside it?"

"None whatsoever, Inspector. My husband and I live here, as I expect Walter has explained, but even when my father is home I rarely come into this room. I don't think I've ever seen the safe open.

"He had it installed about three years ago, soon after he bought the house. I know he used to keep mother's valuables in our old safe, but I'm pretty sure he's given all those away – I have a few pieces, and my sisters and sister-in-law have others. So for all I know, the safe could be empty now!"

"I rather doubt that, madam. If, as we think, this man came a long way to break in, he had reason to believe that there was something in it worth stealing. Or, since it seems clear that he had someone on the inside to help him, that person had actual knowledge of the contents."

"But why would that person then shoot the

burglar before he could open the safe? It doesn't make sense."

"Very true, it doesn't – not yet."

"Have you found out who he is, Inspector?"

"No – my Sergeant is on his way to London as we speak, to make enquiries. We hope to be able to identify the man quite soon."

Tallis returned, carrying a square of tarpaulin. "Got this from one of the gardeners," he reported, laying it down over the stains on the carpet.

"Oh," he added, "we've decided to call off the celebration, and a couple of the guests are thinking of leaving. I've advised them that I don't think that will be permitted – is that right?"

"Absolutely correct, sir. Nobody is to leave the house until I've seen them. And perhaps not even then. I'd appreciate it if you will go and pass that message to everyone. That applies to the family members as well, of course."

Tallis nodded and left again.

"Now, Mrs Burgess, tell me a little about the six guests. All I have at present is a list of names. Are they all friends of all four of you siblings, or has each one perhaps just been invited by a single family member?"

Patricia looked at the Inspector, thinking of the conversation she had with Walter a little earlier. She smiled as she came to a decision. Misguided loyalty to the guests was out of the question.

"The latter, really. No one person of the six is a close friend of all of us. And I must be honest – I personally don't even like a couple of them. You'll need to speak to the other members of the family – including our spouses – but I think everyone will admit to something of a dislike of one or more of the guests. You probably think that's a rather odd situation, but Father said – when he was expecting to be here – that each of the eight of us should invite one guest. If a guest was married he or she could bring their partner, and that would only count as one person. As it happened, none of those invited nominated chose to bring a partner – either because they don't currently have one, or because they chose not to bring their other half.

"Father didn't spell it out, but I inferred that he wanted a few spats to enliven the gathering.

"Anyway, I can tell you who invited whom." Rees picked up his pocketbook and pencil from the table beside him.

"I didn't invite anyone; nor did Walter's wife Jill. Walter invited Eustace Beaumont. My husband Cornelius invited Jonathan Payne. Charity invited Bruce Leach. Her husband Norman Carey invited Cissie Saunders. Emily invited Maurice Todd. Her husband Craig Starling invited Cora McBride."

Rees contemplated what he had written.

"Forgive me, madam, but can I enquire delicately what sort of friends these are? For example, to an outsider it seems a bit odd that two of your married sisters each invited a single male, and two of your brothers-in-law each invited a single female."

Patricia gave a wry smile. "It may be odd to you as an outsider, Inspector, but I can assure you that two or three of the invitations look odd to me too! You may find it even more strange when you see that one or two of these guests are a good ten years younger than the person issuing the invitation.

"But as to 'what sort of friends they are', you must ask those doing the inviting to explain – and of course you'll see the guests and form your own opinions. I can understand some of the invitations, but not all.

"There is one other thing. Father had also invited a guest – Meredith Hammond, who is really his right-hand man. His 'fixer', I think the term is. But when Father found he had to go off unexpectedly, Meredith asked to be excused.

"Now, if you don't have any more questions, I need to start acting as the hostess. Unless you to intend to disappear very soon, I'll arrange for Cook to get some food brought in here for you. Would sandwiches be suitable, or would you prefer something hot?"

"Very kind of you, madam – sandwiches would be fine. Perhaps first I could just see the next person your husband has arranged for me."

"Certainly, Inspector. If you want anything else at any time, just ring the bell. Oh, and if you turn left on leaving the study, the cloakroom is the next door on the right."

Patricia left the room, and Rees returned to his armchair to think.

CHAPTER 7

Left on his own, the DI suddenly remembered that he hadn't considered how the man had travelled to the house. The nearest railway station was over three miles away. Would a burglar come by train? It didn't seem very likely. And there was the ignition key. Almost certainly a car, then. He sighed, and went back to the telephone. Contacting his police station, he learned that Constable Pardoe was not only still in the building, but was actually at the front desk talking to the Superintendent. A minute later, the Super picked up the telephone himself.

"Right, Rees. I've arranged for the gun to be checked, and for the records to be searched. But do you know who the man is yet?"

"No sir. Knowles will call from the Yard if he gets a match from the prints or the face."

"Very well. What do you need now?"

"I need Pardoe again, sir. I want a search for a car which might have brought the dead man to the house. So I'd like Pardoe to do that – go around all the roads nearby. It's his patch, so he knows the area. Starting close to the house, and working outwards. Maybe hidden in a wood, or something, but it can't be far from a road. Pardoe has my car, so he's mobile."

Foster grunted something which Rees took to be assent, and hung up.

The DI didn't have time for any more thinking, as the next interviewee arrived, and he stood to greet her.

He saw an attractive woman of about thirty, with brown hair and a winning smile. Rees was not an expert on female dress, but he thought that the girl's clothes, although smart enough, didn't look expensive.

"I'm Cora McBride," she said, "come to be interrogated."

The DI smiled. "Do sit down," he invited. "Is it Mrs or Miss?"

"Technically Mrs, Inspector, although I don't have much to do with my husband these days."

Rees wasn't too sure how to respond to that, so he ignored it. "You're all here to celebrate Mr Walter Tallis's birthday, I understand. How did you come to be invited?"

"Well, it was out of the blue, really. I know Craig Starling – he's Walter's brother-in-law – because he and I play at the same golf club. We were chatting at the bar one day a couple of weeks ago. He said that his father-in-law had told his son and daughters that both they and their spouses could each invite one acquaintance to this birthday do. 'Invite some odd people to make the occasion a bit more interesting' is apparently what he said.

"Anyway, as we were talking, Craig suddenly said – 'why don't you come?' So I agreed, and here I am. Rather regretting it now, of course."

"So you've never been here before, Mrs McBride?"

"No. Never likely to be invited again, either. The others are mostly nice enough. Of course, Craig's wife Emily looks at me a bit askance, and I suppose that's understandable, but there's never been the slightest thing between her husband and me.

"But there's a funny sort of atmosphere. And I don't just mean since this body was found. I arrived yesterday afternoon, and I haven't felt comfortable since."

"Had you met any of the other five guests before?"

"No; and I hadn't met the other family members either. Oddly enough, I did meet Lord Tallis once, nearly a year ago. We both tried to get into the same taxi at New Street station. He was very decent about it, and was going to cede the taxi to me. He looked okay, and so I suggested we share. He then introduced himself. I was going to remind him about the incident and see if he remembered me – but of course he isn't here.

"As far as the other five guests are concerned, they seem a very mixed bunch. Although most of us come from what I suppose are middle-class backgrounds, we don't seem to have anything in common. But perhaps that was Lord

Tallis's intention – to bring in a disparate lot of people to make things interesting."

Cora shook her head slowly.

"Well, Mrs McBride, I don't think I have anything else to ask you. Thank you for your time."

Rees stood up, and Cora followed.

"Can I leave the house now, Inspector? Mr Tallis said we might be allowed to go after you'd seen us."

The DI hesitated. "Not just yet, I'm afraid, Mrs McBride. How did you get here?"

"Oh, that's all right, Inspector – I'm happy to stay. I came in my own little runabout. I'll say 'goodbye' for the time being, and hope you catch this awful murderer quickly."

Cora departed, almost colliding with a diminutive maid arriving at the door. The girl was bearing a tray, on which was a plate of sandwiches and a pot of tea. Beckoning her to come in, Rees indicated that she should put the tray down on the side table by the armchairs.

The girl looked curiously around the room, and her eyes focussed on the tarpaulin on the floor.

"Cor, is that where he was killed, sir? Lizzie found him, and she's not half upset still."

Rees confirmed that the tarpaulin marked the spot, thanked the maid for the refreshments, and sent her on her way.

Ten minutes later, his 'inner man' satisfied by the intake of some excellent roast beef sandwiches, a large piece of Dundee cake, and two cups of strong tea, he switched his mind back to the case.

He was desperately short of assistants. The bovine Pardoe was willing enough, but hardly suitable for helping with the interviews. Had he done the right thing in despatching Knowles to London? Well, only time would tell. For the first time he began to envy the Metropolitan Police. They had many more cases to handle, of course – but there were many officers to deal with them, they had an excellent records system, and since 1935 they had access to a world-class forensic science laboratory. Also, he understood, they enjoyed the output of a large number of both regular and occasional 'narks'.

He sighed again. If Doctor Bailey was correct, it was likely that some corrupt gunsmith had modified the pistol – and perhaps the Met would know – or at least have suspicions about – such a person.

If Knowles was able to confirm that the dead burglar was indeed a Londoner, then perhaps the Chief Constable would be prepared to ask the Yard to look into bent gunsmiths.

His train of thought was interrupted by a knock, and a tall man in his early thirties put his head round the door.

"I say, are you ready for another candidate?" he enquired, "I'm Eustace Beaumont."

Rising to shake hands, Rees confirmed that

he was ready, and introduced himself.

Beaumont was clean-shaven, and blessed with a fine head of wavy almost golden hair. He was smartly if casually dressed in a navy-blue blazer and slacks, a crimson cravat around his neck adding a bright splash of colour.

"Now, sir, I'm trying to understand the background to this gathering, and what I can't fathom yet is the guest list. I've been told that Lord Tallis suggested that members of his family invited someone. But, if you'll forgive my saying so, the six of you seem rather an odd mix. Can you explain?"

"The word you want is 'disparate', Inspector. You're right, of course. Although I've met Lord Tallis many times, and I suppose I know him reasonably well, I'm not privy to his thinking on this. However, after viewing my fellow-guests after we arrived yesterday, I came to the conclusion that he probably knew that the nominations were likely to produce a number of – shall we say – tensions. If that is so, in my view he would have done that for a purpose, although I can't begin to think what that might be."

"I believe you were invited as the guest of Walter Tallis. Do you know Lord Tallis through him?"

"The other way around, actually. I am quite a significant shareholder in a company which uses a lot of Tallis machinery. I'm a non-executive director, in fact. I met Lord Tallis two or three years ago, and we seemed to hit it off – to the extent that he recently offered me a similar directorship on one of his own companies. I've not yet accepted the position. Anyway, he introduced me to Walter, and we have become friends."

"Had you ever met any of the other five guests before?"

Beaumont hesitated. "Some. I had heard all of the other names."

Rees looked at him closely. "In what context, sir?"

Beaumont shook his head. "I really can't tell you that. All I will say is that when you can speak to Lord Tallis, I think he will confirm that he also knew those names, although I don't think he's actually met all of them, either."

"Not very helpful, sir. This is a murder enquiry, you know."

"I appreciate that, Inspector. But I can't think that tittle-tattle – which is all I have – is useful evidence."

"Evidence, no. But it often gives an indication of where we should be looking – pointing us towards stones which we can then lift to see what might be lurking underneath."

"I see that, Inspector, and I'm not unwilling to help. But most of what I have heard comes from Lord Tallis himself, and I'm not prepared to divulge that at this stage."

"You're the second person who has said much the same thing. Do you know Meredith

Hammond, sir?"

"Certainly. We met at university, and I suppose he remains my closest friend. Each of us was best man at the other's wedding. We play golf together at least once a month. Ah – I guess it's he who has been unwilling to discuss whatever he had heard. Well, that's hardly surprising – he's absolutely loyal to the old man, and has the deserved reputation of being as close as an oyster. Wouldn't be doing the job he does, otherwise."

"Probably a pointless question, sir, but do you have any idea what Lord Tallis might keep in his safe? Have you ever seen it open?"

"No to both. I've been to Walter's house several times, but I've only been here once before, a few weeks ago. My visit was notionally to partake in a shoot. Edgar brought me into this room just once during my visit – and that was to discuss his offer of a directorship. I noticed the safe – one can hardly miss it – but it wasn't opened during the hour or so that we sat in here."

"What do you know about firearms, sir?"

"Smooth-barrelled guns, quite a lot. I own three shotguns – a pair by Purdey and a brand-new Beretta over and under. But if, as I suppose, you mean weapons with rifled barrels, particularly pistols, the answer is practically nothing. As a cadet at school I fired a rifle, and cleaned it afterwards, but that's it. I've never even handled a revolver or automatic, let alone fired one. Military Service lapsed in 1920, so I never served in the army."

Beaumont eyed the detective closely. "I gather that you believe the murder was committed by someone currently present in the house – family, guests, or staff. And it doesn't take a genius to work out that we six oddballs must lead the list of suspects, perhaps with the in-laws as also-rans.

"Well, I'm sure you're right! I don't see Walter or his sisters doing this – they're all very comfortably off and would hardly conspire with someone to break into their father's safe to extract money or jewels. I hardly know the staff here, of course, but I can't see Partridge going around looking for a suitable burglar."

"What about the 'also-rans', sir?

"Ah, well. Those are, to extend the racing analogy, the dark horses, Inspector. I know Jill, Walter's wife, of course, but I simply don't know the others – met them for the first time yesterday.

Beaumont looked out of the window for a moment, almost as though he were looking through the hole in the glass. Bringing his gaze back to Rees, he said:

"I was also going to say that I couldn't imagine Partridge going around trying to buy a pistol – as indeed I couldn't. However, Walter told us that this gun had been specially adapted to take a silencer. I, and probably everyone else who heard that, assumed that this weapon was purchased from some criminal. But something else occurs to me, as perhaps it has to you.

"What if the pistol was in fact already owned by the murderer? It might be quite easy to buy the silencer thing, which I presume is already threaded. All he would have to do would be to get someone with a set of dies to cut an equivalent thread on the end of the barrel. Anyone with the right tools could do this – you wouldn't need an expert gunsmith. In fact, without wanting to make you target me as chief suspect, it's a job I could manage myself in my own workshop at home. Half an hour at most."

Rees looked at Beaumont for a moment, and then smiled.

"I'm obliged to you, sir. Yes, we'll have to see who might have already been in possession of such a pistol.

"Anyway, that's all, as far as I'm concerned, but I'm asking everyone to stay in the house for the time being."

Beaumont shook hands again, and left the room. Rees returned to his chair, and considered this latest theory. He mentally berated himself for not taking the possibility into account already. Clearly, Beaumont was correct in thinking that it must be far easier to buy a silencer than to buy an unlicensed gun.

Doctor Bailey had said that Webley pistols of this sort were very common. The inference, the DI thought, was that they were issued during the War. If that was right, then perhaps he should concentrate on those of an age to have served.

However, attractive as this theory was, it still didn't eliminate the possibility that the gun and silencer had been bought together.

He sighed, just as there was another knock on the door. A burly man of about forty, dressed in tweeds, and with black hair and a moustache, came in.

He introduced himself as Bruce Leach. Rees knew from his list that he was an 'honourable' – in other words he was, like Walter Tallis, the son of a member of the peerage.

The two men sat down, and the DI started off as he had done with Beaumont. Leach confessed to being surprised that Charity had invited him.

"I've known her for years," he said; "her husband Norman too. Don't jump to conclusions, but twelve or so years ago I suppose Norman and I were rivals for her hand.

"Anyway, our respective daughters were at a gymkhana a month or so ago, and while we were watching the jumping, out of the blue she asked me to come to Walter's birthday party.

"She told me that her father – I've met him a few times, by the way, and stayed here before – had told all his family to invite someone – and that if that person didn't get on with other people it would make it more interesting.

"Well, I'm not sure if I'm flattered to be included in that category. As the son of a peer I can pass muster anywhere, but I have to admit that

I never worry about not making friends, and so I do have a tendency to say things sometimes which upset people."

"How many of those present this week have you met before, sir?"

Leach considered. "Charity and Norman, as I said. Walter and his wife a couple of times. Pat and Cornelius – they live here, so I've met them when I've been a guest here before. I hadn't met the other sister or her husband. I've heard of Todd and Beaumont, but although we might have been in the same room at some function, I don't think we'd ever spoken. I know of Payne, although we're never met. Never come across the two women before. Payne's all right, and Cora seems very nice, but frankly, I don't want to see Todd or the Saunders woman again after this."

Rees changed tack. "Did you serve in the war, sir?"

"Yes, I did, Inspector. I was commissioned into the Royal Field Artillery in 1916. After training, I served, without any special distinction, in France and Belgium. I was discharged in early 1919.

"You want to know if I can shoot, I presume. Well, I suppose the answer must be 'yes'."

"A bit more than that, sir. Did you carry a sidearm?"

"Oh, yes, of course. I was issued with a heavy service revolver, but was never very good with it. So I wangled a self-loading pistol made by the same company. Quite liked that. Then, like many others, I acquired a Luger from a captured German. Beautiful gun. But although the army supplied ammunition for both the Webleys, 9-millimetre stuff wasn't readily available, unless occasionally some was taken off a captured – or dead – German. So I didn't actually carry the Luger anywhere near the front line. Does that help, Inspector?"

"I really don't know, sir. Do you still have these pistols?"

"I still have the Luger somewhere, although I haven't seen it for years. As for the heavy revolver and the Webley automatic, I suppose they were returned to stores when I left the service. It's eighteen years ago, and I don't remember any detail."

"If you don't have a certificate, you're in breach of the Firearms Act. In fact you needed one in 1920, and should then have renewed it every three years. Three months in prison is the penalty, I think."

The telephone rang, but Rees ignored it, and it quickly stopped.

"Sorry to disappoint you, Inspector. I gave notice to the Chief Constable in 1920 that the Luger was a 'trophy of war' under Section 13 of the Act, and he gave me written dispensation that a certificate was not required. As far as I know, that dispensation remains in force indefinitely. True, I'm not allowed to have ammunition for the thing."

Rees admitted that he was unaware of this obscure provision of the law. He thought again for a minute.

"The safe over there, sir. Have you ever seen it open, or have you ever heard Lord Tallis or anyone else say what might be inside it?"

"No to both questions. Until I came in here to see you just now, I'd never set foot in the room. Indeed, until Walter told us about this burglar chap, I didn't even know there was a safe in the house. And I shouldn't have expected his father to tell me anything about the contents. I don't think he likes me, for a start."

Rees had just decided to end the interview, when there was another knock at the door. To the DI's call of come in, the Butler appeared.

"Two things, sir," he intoned in a very deep voice. "First, Constable Pardoe is here and wishes to see you. Second, there is a telephone call for you – from London, I understand. If you pick up the receiver on the desk, you'll be connected, and I'll hang up the other instrument."

As Rees moved to the desk, Pardoe came into the room, clutching his helmet. Partridge retired, closing the door behind him.

Signalling Pardoe to stay where he was, Rees picked up the telephone. An excited voice started talking from the other end of the line, and the DI sharply told him to wait for a minute. Seconds later, a click told him that the other receiver had been put down.

"Right Knowles, what have you found?" asked Rees.

"He's Danny Skinner, sir. They've got prints and a mugshot here, and there's no doubt. He's done time for burglary and safe-breaking – came out about a year ago after a six-year stretch. I've spoken to a DS in CID, and he says they've had suspicions about him ever since he came out, but haven't been able to pin anything on him.

"Oh, and they tell me he works alone – told the DI who went to question him recently that he was 'grassed up' once and will never trust anyone again.

"Just one other thing sir. The rumour is that he has always worked on commission, so to speak. He was caught last time because of an unfortunate accident – unfortunate from his point of view, anyway. The things he was caught with would have been almost impossible to fence, and it was believed he was acting on behalf of some private collector who would gloat over the items behind locked doors."

"Good; well done Sergeant. Just hang on a minute while I speak to Pardoe. What have you got, Pardoe?"

Found a car sir. At the edge of a wood not a hundred yards from the end of the drive of this house. It's a big Lanchester. No sign of anyone around, sir, and the engine is cold."

"Right. That sounds like our man's car. Give me the number."

Pardoe handed over his pocket book, open at the current page. Rees dictated the registration number to Knowles, and told him to ask the Yard people to find the owner. "Ask politely, Knowles – this isn't their case so they aren't obliged to be helpful. Call me again when you have any information.

"Pardoe, take this key, walk back to the Lanchester, and – assuming the key fits – drive the car back here. Bring the key back to me, and then go back to normal duties."

He turned back to Leach. "Just one more question, sir. Do you know a man named Danny Skinner?"

"Doesn't ring a bell, Inspector. And if that's the burglar chap, well, I don't move in those circles.

"Unless you have any more questions, I'll go."

CHAPTER 8

Before the DI could settle in his chair again to have a think, there was another visitor.

Cissie Saunders seemed to be even younger than Cora McBride. She had blonde hair – or at least apparently blonde, thought Rees (who although a bachelor had heard that there was such a thing as hair dye). She was dressed in a simple white blouse and navy-blue skirt. Some men might have described her as pretty, but DI thought she had rather a hard face which rendered her less attractive. 'Knowing' was the word which came to his mind. She wore no rings, nor indeed any other jewellery.

"Do sit down, Miss Saunders. Now, this won't take us very long. No doubt you've heard all about what's happened here."

"Sure, Inspector. Walter has given us what I think is called the 'lowdown'.

She smiled, but Rees thought it didn't really look genuine. What surprised him was that the woman spoke with a distinct accent. Cockney, he thought. He wasn't an expert in such things, and was wrong, although not by many miles. In fact Cissie had been born and raised in Peckham.

"How did you come to be invited to this

gathering, Miss Saunders?"

"Funny thing, really. I work for Norman Carey, in London. Norman is the husband of one of Lord Tallis's daughters. Anyway, about a fortnight ago, he mentioned that his father-in-law had told his relatives to invite just one person to his son's birthday party. And Norman said that each of these people was to be 'different' somehow.

I asked who he was going to invite. He said he hadn't decided, so I jokingly said that if he invited me I'd jump at the chance of being a proper guest in some lord's mansion. And Norman said 'good idea – you must come.'

"So that's what happened. It was a mistake, I guess. Everyone is polite and everything. A few people are really nice – Mr Burgess and Mr Beaumont especially, and Mr Tallis too. But some of the family – and a couple of the other guests – are very snobby, and I know they look down on me. What's worse is that Norman seems to regret inviting me – he's hardly spoken to me since I arrived. And Charity – Norman's wife doesn't speak to me at all. I suppose she thinks I'm Norman's mistress, or something."

"Are you?"

Cissie smiled for the first time. "No. Oh, I admit we've had a kiss and a cuddle in the office sometimes, but no more than that."

"Do you know a man named Danny Skinner?"

"There were some Skinners in our street

when I was a kid, but I don't remember a Danny then or since. Why?"

"It's the name of the dead man. Ever fired a gun?"

"No. Oh, I've had a go at a fairground on one of those stalls where you shoot at a target and might win some cheap prize – but they aren't real guns, are they? Air guns or something like that. Anyway, I'm useless."

"Had Mr Carey ever mentioned his father-in-law to you before?"

"Yeah, several times. On the one hand he seemed to be pleased to have married into a titled family – Charity is an 'honourable', of course – but on the other hand he didn't seem to like Lord Tallis. Made a few nasty remarks about him, but I never understood what his grouse was."

"Very well, Miss Saunders, that's all. Did you come here by train?"

"No, Inspector – Norman brought me in his car."

"Well, I want everyone to stick around for a bit longer."

"Don't expect he'll want to take me back anyway," she remarked as she opened the door. "I'll maybe ask one of the others to take me to the station when you've finished with us."

Cornelius Burgess heard this as he stood aside to let her leave. "I'll be happy to drive you to the station – either the local one or New Street as you wish – when or if the Inspector releases us."

"Oh, thank you so much, Mr Burgess – I'd be so grateful."

Burgess came into the study, closed the door behind him, and shook hands with Rees. The DI indicated the armchairs, but was interrupted by the telephone. This time he decided to pick it up. He gave his name and listened.

"I see. From where? When? Doesn't really help, but well done, Knowles. Final job while you're there. Just see if the CID people would ask around to see if anyone knows of a gunsmith who might not be averse to working on an illegal pistol – grinding off serial numbers, fitting a silencer, that sort of thing. When you've done that, get back here as soon as you can. Best go straight home, as you won't get back before I've left here. I'll see you at the station in the morning, and I'll fill you in as we drive back here."

Rees replaced the receiver, and sat down with Burgess.

"Apologies, sir – that was my Sergeant calling from Scotland Yard. Seems the car our dead man arrived in was stolen only a few hours before he was killed.

"His name is Skinner, by the way – Danny Skinner. Does that mean anything to you?"

"Sorry, absolutely nothing, Inspector. I don't think I've ever met a Skinner."

"I've been hearing about this birthday gathering, sir – and in particular about the unusual arrangement for inviting guests. You invited Mr Payne, I understand?"

"That's right, he is my invitee. And you're right again – the whole set-up is very odd. I didn't actually hear Edgar suggest this guest business – Pat told me about it. She wasn't very happy, actually, because as hostess she'd have to arrange for bedrooms and so on and she though that might be a bit tricky for people that she might not know. Also, she felt that a private birthday party wasn't really the time to bring in a number of people who themselves might not know more than one other person. But her father, for whatever reason, was adamant. And apparently pushed the point about avoiding 'safe' people. Sorry, Inspector, that wasn't meant to be a pun.

"Anyway, Pat decided not to issue her invitation card, but she insisted that I must do so myself. I cast around in my mind for someone who might fulfil Edgar's wish, as that wish had been reported to me. Eventually I chose Jonathan Payne. He is an extremely bright chap, who is doing very well after a poor start in life. Raised in an orphanage, in 1914 he enlisted in one of the 'Pals' battalions of the Royal Warwickshires at the age of seventeen. In two years, he went from private to staff sergeant, and was then commissioned in the field. A remarkable achievement in itself. Then, discharged as a captain, he managed to become an articled clerk with a firm of Birmingham solicitors. Took him over seven years, but he eventually qualified.

"I came across him a couple of years ago, when his firm did some work for us. I liked 'the cut of his jib'. Not long after that, Edgar and I were discussing having a few in-house solicitors rather than going to other firms all the time. I mentioned Payne, and after meeting him – in this house, actually – Edgar offered him a job. At present Payne is on the same footing as Hammond, of whom I expect you've heard – employed by Edgar personally, not by one of the companies. But the experiment has been successful, and the plan now is that the role will be expanded over the next few months, and Payne will then head up a legal team for the benefit of all five Tallis companies. At that stage he might be transferred into one of the existing companies – probably one in which I'm Finance Director – or the legal team might be floated as a separate company.

"You probably didn't need all that background, but basically I invited him because not only is he a very nice unassuming chap, but both Edgar and Walter like him."

"It's all useful material, sir. We gather up all these little snippets, and some of them may prove to be vital.

"What about your own war service?"

"I thought you'd get on to that. It's the pistol, I suppose. Yes, I was in the Army. I had a Special Reserve commission pre-war, and in 1914 I went straight in as a captain. I had an odd war, I suppose. I was lucky enough to avoid France, but I saw active service in the Dardanelles – where again I was incredibly lucky in that I wasn't even injured – and later with Allenby in Palestine.

"Yes, I carried a sidearm – a Webley service revolver. I handed it in after the war ended, and I haven't touched a handgun since."

"Thank you sir, very clear. Let's go back to the other guests, if you will. How many did you know before they arrived?"

Burgess thought for a moment.

"I'd met Leach – he came to stay here once. I've known Beaumont for several years – and he's stayed here before too. Hadn't met Todd, although his name seemed vaguely familiar. Never met or indeed heard of either of the women."

"You think you'd come across Todd's name – can you have another think and see if you can remember where?"

"I'll try again, Inspector, but this has been niggling me ever since we arrived. I just haven't been able to pin my memory down. And before you ask, I have no idea whether my vague memory of him – if it has any basis at all – will be about something which is to his credit, or otherwise."

"I understand, sir. Now, it wouldn't be appropriate to ask you to comment on the family members. You all seem to be comfortably off, and it seems unlikely that any of you eight would need to raid the safe. But I think I can decently ask you to comment on your fellow guests – just your opinions of the ones you didn't know from your observations over the last couple of days."

Burgess looked at the DI, then shifted his gaze to the hole in the window just as Beaumont had done earlier. Looking back at Rees, he sighed.

"Payne, obviously, I should trust absolutely. Likewise Beaumont. I'd need a longer acquaintance to decide on Mrs McBride, but provisionally she seems okay. The remaining three, frankly, I don't want to spend any more time with. Terrible thing to say, and perhaps quite unfair, but I shouldn't agree to lend any of them a half-crown."

Rees smiled to himself. He himself tended to make quick judgements about people, and believed that his own intuition in this respect was valid. He therefore respected the view of Burgess, whose education and intellect was, he knew, superior to his own.

But Burgess hadn't quite finished. "Look, Inspector, it's not, as you say, for me to comment on the family members. However, it's very unfortunate that Edgar is away. Within these four walls, I'll say this. I rather think that if you put a question to him about his family, you might hear one or two adverse comments."

Rees nodded slowly. "I see; yes, there have been one or two similar hints. Well, I'm going to try to contact Lord Tallis by wireless, although I certainly can't expect him to make comments on the open airwaves!"

"Just one more point that I've been thinking

about, Inspector. Both Walter and Pat, when reporting this to the rest of us, said that the safe was locked. From that, they seem to assume that this Skinner man hadn't managed to open it before being killed.

"That seems very unlikely to me. If, as everyone seems to believe, he was shot by an accomplice, that implies that the inside person commissioned Skinner to open the safe. It also implies that the insider doesn't possess the necessary skill to do the job. Therefore, why on earth would he – or she – kill Skinner before the safe was opened?

"No. I suggest he was killed *after* he'd done the job. The loot was then taken, and the safe locked again. One only has to turn the handle to shoot the bolts, and then spin the combination dial."

"You may well have a point, sir," replied the DI, who realised that he really should have considered this possibility from the start. "Trouble is, until we know what was in the safe, and then get it open to see if anything is missing, we're in the dark. Suppose a load of jewellery is missing. I could search the house – something your wife has already given authority for – but I have no idea what to look for. In a place this size a search for small objects would take an army and weeks to complete anyway. Even more hopeless to search for money," he added gloomily.

As Burgess left the room, a footman who

had apparently been waiting outside came in and handed over the car key. "Constable Pardoe asked me to give you this, sir. The car is parked around the side."

The DI considered having the car checked for prints, but decided that would be pointless. However, he did find his way out of the house and went to check to see if any clue might have been left inside. As he expected, there was nothing. Making his way back into the house via the back door, after passing through a scullery he found himself in a huge kitchen which appeared to double as the servants' hall. Here he encountered the Cook, a cheerful-looking woman of about fifty. Being tall and spare she was quite unlike his vision of what someone in this position would look like. Quickly introducing himself, Rees thanked her for his sandwiches. He returned to the study in time to greet the next interviewee.

CHAPTER 9

"Good afternoon Inspector, I'm Jonathan Payne," announced the newcomer, offering his hand.

"Come and sit down, sir," invited Rees. He directed the visitor to an armchair as before.

"First, and probably a pointless question, have you heard of a man named Danny – presumably Daniel – Skinner?"

"I haven't, no. Is that the dead burglar?"

"It is. Now, I've been hearing a lot about the selection of guests for Mr Tallis's birthday. I understand you were invited by Mr Burgess, and he has explained why you were picked. He has given you what I might call a very good write-up – so good in fact that one almost becomes suspicious!"

Payne grinned. "How embarrassing! Well, it wasn't me wot dunnit. I've been hearing about your questions, so I'll answer them as far as I can without needing to have them put to me.

"No, I have no idea about the contents of the safe. I knew it was here – I've been in this study once before, for a chat with Lord Tallis. But the safe wasn't even mentioned, let alone opened in my presence.

"Yes, I can handle a pistol – I used to be quite a good shot, as it happens. But I haven't touched any firearm except a shotgun for nearly twenty years. I don't possess a handgun – legally or illegally.

"Of the other thirteen people here this week, I knew all four of the Tallis clan, plus Jill and of course Cornelius. I'd also met Beaumont several times. I'd never met Starling or Carey – they don't have any role in the businesses, and neither was here on my only previous visit. I'd heard of Todd and Leach, but I don't recall ever meeting them. I'd never come across either of the two women."

"I'll be honest, sir," said Rees. "I have practically no experience in a case of murder. Nor, for that matter, in a case where a good number of the suspects are from what we might call the top drawer. I want to ask Mr Tallis and his sisters about each other – and more particularly the others' spouses, but I really can't do that. I have tried to ask about the guests."

Rees paused, and looked expressionlessly at the solicitor. Payne smiled.

"I should never speak ill of the direct family, Inspector. They are effectively my employers, after all. However, hand on heart, I can say that I would have nothing adverse to say about any of them anyway. Nor about Cornelius and Jill.

"Strictly within these four walls, that loyalty might not extend to the other spouses. As I said, I'd never met Starling or Carey. On admittedly very little acquaintance, I've not taken to either of them. Starling appears a boastful type, although what he has to boast about apart from hooking Charity and thus a meal-ticket for life, I'm not sure. I don't even know what, if anything, he does. Carey is supposed to be 'in finance' in the City of London. All I'd say is I should never entrust him with a penny of my money. Carey Street is of course where the bankruptcy courts used to be, so perhaps my mistrust is only based on his name.

"I have no loyalty at all to my fellow-guests. Eustace Beaumont is a first-rate chap; I've nothing against him. I've managed to develop an active dislike of Leach and Todd, which I admit might have been triggered by the rumours I've heard about them.

"I feel sorry for Cissie. I can empathise with her – I wasn't born into this sort of life either. She, poor girl, wasn't blest with the brains to pull her upwards – although I imagine she's done her best with her body. There is something slightly off-putting about her, although I can't explain that feeling. I haven't thought 'I'd like to invite you to dinner', which I have in the case of Cora. Indeed, as I gather she is separated and awaiting a divorce, I may well try that – she seems a nice girl.

"There, Inspector, I've been as honest as I can be!"

"Thank you, sir. I appreciate all that. Personal opinions aren't evidence, of course, but I've always found that gut feeling can often prove accurate."

Both men sat quietly for a minute. The

telephone rang, but the DI ignored it again.

"As a solicitor, my job largely consists of offering advice. Mine to you, Inspector, is to contact Lord Tallis as soon as you can. I have a feeling that you won't get anywhere near to solving this case until you do."

Rees looked even more despondent. "I'm going to do that shortly. But it won't be possible to have a private conversation with him on the *Ile de France* – and even in the unlikely event that he turned round and returned by the next ship it would be a week before he could be back here."

There was a tap at the door, and Partridge appeared. "A telephone call for you sir," he announced.

"I'll leave you, Inspector," said Payne. "I'm not asking to leave today, so I'll be available to answer more questions if you think of any."

When the door closed, the DI picked up the telephone again. It was, as he had anticipated, Sergeant Knowles.

"I'm still here, sir. I've been talking to various officers. They know of a couple of dodgy gunsmiths – that is people with mainly legitimate businesses who are rumoured to supply under-the-counter weapons from time to time. One in Camberwell, and one in Marylebone. Nothing ever proved in either case.

"The other thing concerns Skinner. He lives in Camden – so not particularly close to either of the gun people. But the car was taken from a house in Camden – within a couple of hundred yards of Skinner's house. The stupid owner admits that when he parked on his drive he often left the ignition key in the car.

"Do you want to ask any more about anything, sir? I don't think there's much the Met can do about the gun at present."

"Agreed. But you can organise one other thing. Someone there will know how to do this. I want to send a message to a ship in the middle of the Atlantic – the *Ile de France*. I have no idea if you can have a voice connection, but I assume this'll have to be via Morse code.

"Write this down, Knowles. Message is for Viscount Tallis in person. Marked 'confidential', if that's possible. The essence of the message is this:

"Safebreaker found shot dead in your study beside safe. Assailant unknown but believed to be an occupant of your house. Uncertain whether safe was opened. Please advise what safe contains. Also if you are willing to divulge combination either to police or your son. Reply to Worcester police – give my name and the station number, Knowles.

"I assume you can telephone that to some radio transmitting station. Obviously that'll cost a bit – if the charge is put on the Yard number you call from, promise that they can bill us later. Have you got all that, or do you want me to repeat it?"

Knowles confirmed that he had noted everything, including the name of the ship, and the call ended.

Rees stood and stared out of the window for a few minutes. He felt somewhat overwhelmed. He wanted someone to talk to about the case. Even Sergeant Knowles, who couldn't be called an intellectual, would have been good. Certainly, he could talk about the facts with some of the suspects – and had in fact done so. Indeed, perhaps he had said more than was wise. But he told himself that some of the suspects were less suspect than others.

An icy wind was blowing through the circular hole in the French window. It had been doing that all day, in fact, but he hadn't noticed until now. He decided that he would take up Mrs Burgess's offer, and pressed the bell push beside the desk. The same maid who had brought his refreshments arrived within a minute.

"Yes, sir?" she enquired, her gaze flickering between the Inspector and the tarpaulin on the floor.

Rees indicated the hole in the window. "See what you can find to block up that hole, please. If there is any of that new-fangled sticky Scotch tape in the house, someone could fasten a sheet of cardboard over the hole. Failing that, a screwed-up newspaper might do the trick. I just need a temporary fix until the glass can be repaired properly. What's your name, by the way?"

"I'm Trixie, sir – Beatrix. I think Mr Partridge may have some of that sticky stuff. I'll go and ask."

Rees moved away from the window and shivered. The temperature probably hadn't altered much in the room all day, but noticing the draught had somehow made it worse.

He wondered who his next interviewee would be, and mentally bet that it would be another guest. However, the next person to come in was Partridge, accompanied by a footman. Another man followed closely behind.

"Please do the best you can with that hole, Partridge," instructed Rees.

"Now sir," he addressed the third man, "I'm Detective Inspector Rees – who are you?"

The DI lost his mental bet, because the newcomer introduced himself as Norman Carey. The two men shook hands, sat down, and looked at each other.

Rees saw another man of about forty, dressed in a similar fashion to Beaumont – in blazer and slacks, but with a conventional magenta tie rather than a cravat. He was clean-shaven, with thinning fair hair, and wore gold-rimmed spectacles.

"Well, Inspector, I suppose you have to wait until Partridge and Wells leave the room before starting the third-degree stuff," he smiled.

"That's right, sir – we don't want witnesses.

The Butler had his back to the two seated men, and so they couldn't see his face. Had they been able to do so, neither would have had any trouble in interpreting his expression.

Partridge was mentally enjoying the thought of Carey being beaten up by a corrupt police officer with a rubber truncheon or something similar. For a moment he wished that this Inspector would do something like that, after which he himself could deny witnessing anything. He was pretty sure that Mason, the footman, would also choose to turn a blind eye. Partridge quickly wiped this inappropriate thought from his mind, and continued to supervise the work on the window. This didn't take long, and Rees thanked the two servants as they withdrew.

"Now sir, just a few questions. No third degree, I'm afraid – it's frowned on these days.

"You are married to Charity, I believe. How long have you been in the family?"

"About seven years, Inspector. Charity is the second of Tallis's children – Pat is the eldest, then Charity, then Walter, and Emma is the youngest. I'm a couple of years younger than my wife.

"Do you get on with the other family members?"

Carey looked surprised at the question, and hesitated. "Well enough, I suppose. I don't say that I'd choose Walter or Cornelius as drinking companions, and Pat isn't my favourite female, but we don't have rows or anything."

"What about Lord Tallis?"

Carey scowled. "I'll be perfectly frank. He's never said anything in the seven or eight years I've known him, but I'm pretty sure he has always thought that I'm not good enough for his daughter."

"Every father thinks that about his daughter's suitors, surely, sir?"

"Perhaps. But I'd expected to be given a directorship in one of his companies, as Jill and Cornelius have. A few shares as well."

"So what do you do for a living?"

"I have a small company in London, Inspector. We provide financial advice – about investments, and so on."

"How is the company doing, sir – would you say you are comfortably off?"

"What on earth has that do with the police?"

"Simple, really. A rich man would have no need to steal from Lord Tallis."

Carey grunted. "We do all right."

"And I understand that your income is supplemented by your wife's directorship in one of her father's companies?"

"That is so, yes. You really are being rather offensive."

"Just doing my job, sir. What do you know about firearms?"

"Not much. I was called up in 1915, and – perhaps because I had some experience in sailing dinghies – was put in the Royal Navy. I then spent the rest of the war in Harwich, organising ship movements, arranging berths, and so on. An embarrassingly safe billet, and often boring. I did some range shooting during initial training, and then I was commissioned. I never really saw a gun after that."

"Surely officers were issued with sidearms, sir?"

"I believe that was so in the Army, but not in the Navy – not to those of us in the port office at Harwich harbour, anyway."

"I see. What do you know about this safe, sir?"

"I knew it was here, of course, although I've only been in this room half a dozen times in as many years. I have no idea what Tallis might keep in it."

"Tell me about the guests. How many of them did you know before this visit?"

"You certainly change tack rapidly, Inspector. Well, I've known Leach for years. I know you've already seen him, and no doubt he told you that he was once my rival for Charity's hand. I don't like the man, but I bear him no grudge – although he may well bear one against me!

"Beaumont stayed here once when I was also in the house. I've heard Payne's name mentioned before, but I'd never previously met him. I didn't know Todd, or the McBride woman. I expect you've been told about Tallis's strange idea of inviting some unusual guests. No doubt Cissie has also told you that she was my invitee. She works for me in London."

"What does your wife think about that invitation, sir?"

Carey flushed. "I can't say."

"Really, sir? I hear that she has pointedly refused to speak to Miss Saunders."

"All right, I admit that Charity isn't happy. It was a mistake to invite Cissie, and I shall have to dismiss her."

"You'll miss the kisses and cuddles in your office."

"That is an outrageous comment, Inspector," responded Carey angrily. "And that just confirms that Cissie will have to go."

"This situation isn't of her making, sir. But another thing. I understand that your wife invited Bruce Leach. I wonder if she did that after she learned that you were inviting your paramour, or whether you invited Miss Saunders after you found your wife was invited her old friend."

Carey flushed again. "I resent the term 'paramour'. Charity did invite Leach, that's true. They've stayed on good terms, Inspector. I don't want to comment any further, except to say that I don't see how any of these relationships are relevant to the murder of some burglar."

"Every little bit of information about the character of a suspect is potentially relevant in a murder case. We look at everything, file it away, and eventually we find out whether it leads anywhere or not. Most of it doesn't, of course.

"Anyway, that's all for the time being, Mr Carey, thank you."

Carey stormed out of the room still visibly

fuming, and slammed the door behind him.

In the small storage room opposite the study door, Partridge smiled. He had deliberately left the study door ajar as he and the footman had left – and had been able to hear Mr Carey's embarrassing interview.

CHAPTER 10

Rees was pacing around the study when the next interviewee arrived. He realised that Tallis must have made the arrangements such that as one person came out, the next on the list was mobilised. Certainly everything was progressing efficiently, even if he couldn't detect any progress in solving the case.

The latest arrival turned out to be the sixth and last of the guests, Maurice Todd.

Todd was a little younger than the two previous men, probably only in his mid-thirties, Rees thought. But despite the advantage of youth, he did not present well. Noting the bleary and indeed bloodshot eyes, the hair in desperate need of a brush, and the tie askew, the word 'dissipated' came unbidden to the DI's mind.

He invited the visitor to take a seat, and started to go through much the same questions as before.

Todd had no military experience, having been too young to take part in the war, and claimed to have never handled any firearm other than the usual shotgun. He had never even been in the house before, let alone the study, and had no idea a safe even existed. He had only met Lord Tallis once, at a party, and admitted that he hadn't made a good impression on the peer.

He had never heard of Danny Skinner. He was acquainted with Bruce Leach – "wouldn't exactly say we are friends" – and had "come across" Eustace Beaumont a few times. He had never met the other three guests.

As far as the family members were concerned, it seemed he had "come across" Walter and Jill Tallis, but had never met the Burgesses or the Careys.

That left the Starlings, and the DI suspected that Todd was reluctant to explain their relationship. Rees asked a direct question.

"Why do you think Emily Starling invited you?"

Todd avoided the Inspector's eye. "Well, she said her father had told everyone to invite odd people – people who might be 'different' rather than just old friends from the same class."

"Aren't you from the same 'class', Mr Todd?"

"Well, I suppose so. But I'm a bit different."

"Explain the difference, if you please."

Todd looked a bit embarrassed. "Well, I'm a lot poorer, for a start. I'm currently out of work."

"What was your job?"

The embarrassment seemed to increase. "I was a solicitor."

"Plenty of work available, surely?"

"Oh, hell," exclaimed Todd. "Here it is. I embezzled some money – not a lot – from a client's account, and I served two years in prison. Lost the job, of course, and was struck off the Law Society's rolls."

"And Mrs Starling knows about this, of course?"

"Yes. Craig and I were good friends at university, and I met Emily many times before they were married. We've kept up ever since – and Emily is one of the few who didn't drop me like a hot potato when I did something stupid."

"What about her husband – what does he think about his wife inviting another man to a birthday party?"

Todd hesitated. "You'll have to ask him. He hasn't said anything to me. Actually, it's just occurred to me that he may not even know that I'm here at her behest.

"But anyway, here's another thing. I do know that Craig invited that lovely girl Cora McBride. I'd never even heard of her, but Craig has produced her from somewhere."

"Are you implying that Mr Starling invited her in retaliation for his wife inviting you?"

"I'm not saying that, but I suppose it is possible."

"Let's go back to your financial state. Obviously, the richer someone is, the less likely it is that they need to burgle someone else's safe. You'll appreciate that most of the people here – both family and visitors – might be called comfortably off. And someone who already has a criminal record might be more likely to commit an offence than someone with no previous convictions."

"I can't deny any of that, Inspector. No doubt you're also thinking that I must have met burglars when I was serving my sentence. I probably did, although most people kept silent about what they were inside for. But I assure you that I didn't, as far as I know, meet a safebreaker."

"Did you do your time in London?"

"No, in Winson Green. I haven't been to London for years."

"Does Mrs Starling help you financially?"

Todd flushed. "She has helped me out three or four times in the last few months."

"Detail, please?"

"A hundred pounds once. Fifty a couple of times. A few tenners."

"One final question, just for my own interest, really. Do you regret joining this party?"

Todd considered the question. "Until I came into this room, the answer would have been 'no', Inspector. Even though there seem to have been some odd interactions between some of the people, I've enjoyed a bit of social life, which for me has been rather absent recently.

"But the embarrassment of having to bare my soul to you has rather taken the shine of the visit. Overall, though, I think the experience remains positive."

"Give me some examples of 'odd

interactions'."

"Well, I haven't really understood why, but the Careys hardly seem to be on speaking terms – and Norman Carey doesn't speak to the woman he apparently invited. Also, I know it was Craig who invited Cora, but he seems to be avoiding her and it's the Payne chap who's been talking to her the most.

"Incidentally, Payne is a solicitor and must know of my peccadillo, but he's been very decent and not mentioned it during conversations."

"All right, sir, that's all I want to ask you. But I'm asking everyone not to leave the house for the time being."

Todd smiled for the first time. "I'll probably stay for as long as Patricia will put up with me. The food is good, and quite a bit of the company is charming.

"It's rather horrible being suspected of murder, but I have a clean conscience. You seem to be convinced that the killer is neither an outsider nor a servant, Inspector. So I suppose there's a certain *frisson* in watching everyone else to see who might give a clue as to their guilt."

Almost as soon as Todd had left the room, Mrs Tallis returned.

"Time's getting on, Inspector, and you must be hungry again. Assuming you've here a while longer, can I tempt you with clear soup followed by some shepherd's pie? In about half an hour?"

Very kind, ma'am. I do want to see the

remaining four people tonight. But rather than hot food I wonder if your cook could just find a few more of her excellent sandwiches?"

"Certainly. You had beef for lunch, I think. Would you like ham, or egg, or more beef, or a variety?"

"A variety sounds most appealing, ma'am, thank you."

At the door, Patricia almost collided with the next interviewee. With an apology, he stepped aside to let her pass.

CHAPTER 11

As only one male remained on his list, it didn't take a lot of deductive skill to identify the newcomer as Craig Starling. He saw a handsome man, over six feet tall, well-groomed, and perhaps just on the right side of forty. After mutual introductions, the two men sat down. The DI wondered how best to play this interview. Clearly there were family tensions, but whether these were in any way relevant was yet to be ascertained. However, Starling immediately helped by tackling the matter head-on.

"You want to know about Emily, Maurice, Cora, and me," he said.

"Well, it's messy, and that doesn't reflect well on me. I've long been jealous of Maurice, irrationally, probably. He and I became friends nearly twenty years ago, although he's been away for a couple of years and it's only in the last few weeks we've picked up again. I know he's seen Emily several times lately. I'm well aware, although I've said nothing to either of them, that she invited him here this week. So – and I freely admit I was stupid – I used my invitation card on Cora. Thing is, I think Em was sorry for Maurice, rather than in love with him or anything like that.

She and I haven't managed to talk privately about the situation yet, but I'm confident that we can sort it out.

"Cora is the wife of someone I do some business with – although they're soon to be divorced. There has never been anything between us. We are members of the same golf club, but we've never even played a round together." Starling realised the ambiguity of what he had said, and smiled apologetically – "you know what I mean."

"Thank you for being so frank, sir. However, you don't need to be quite so cagey – I know where Mr Todd spent those two years. "Let's talk about firearms. Did you see any service in the war?"

"Towards the end, yes. I was only sixteen and still at school when it broke out. I joined up in 1917, and was commissioned within a month or so. After training, I was posted to France. I was involved at St Quentin, and in the Second Battle of Cambrai.

"Anticipating your next question, yes, I was issued with a sidearm. One of those heavy Webley revolvers. Fine for close encounters in a trench, certainly – lots of stopping power – but pretty useless at more than fifteen or twenty yards. But I hear this chap was killed with an automatic, and I can say hand on heart that I've never fired one."

"Going back to the house guests. How many did you know prior to this week?"

"Maurice and Cora, obviously. Never heard

of Cissie. I know Beaumont quite well – we're both members of a club in Birmingham and of another in London. I've met Leach a few times, but we certainly aren't friends. I know Payne slightly – he was here once when Em and I were staying in the house.

"I should explain – although you probably know this already – that I have no role in any of the Tallis companies. If I did, I guess I'd know Payne far better – and indeed my brothers-in-law Walter and Cornelius too.

"And yes, I rather resent the fact that I've not been given a directorship, although I'm not alone – Norman is in the same position. But please don't assume that I bear Tallis a grudge so huge that I'd want to steal from his safe. I'm not a poor man in my own right, and my wife nets quite a bit from her position in the company."

Rees leaned back in his armchair and closed his eyes.

"We're working on the assumption that the burglar was specially commissioned for this job. He was a London man named Skinner, by the way, and known to the police down there. We also assume that he was killed by the person who hired him – we don't yet know why.

"But it has to be an insider. A member of the family, a guest, or a servant. Frankly, it's impossible to believe that one of the servants would have the wherewithal to hire a professional safebreaker. Nor to have the knowledge to make enquiries around the seedier parts of London in order to find such a person.

"No – the killer is either a guest or a member of the Tallis family."

Opening his eyes, and looking straight at the other man, the DI asked:

"Who is your money on, sir?"

Taken aback, Starling stared back at the Inspector, his lips moving without any words coming out.

"I can't help thinking that's an improper question," he said at last. "I have absolutely no idea who it is, although I quite see your logic in plumping for it being one of us.

"However, trying to think logically myself, it would seem likely that this safe man must have been arranged well in advance. I can't imagine that someone who received his invitation in the last couple of days – if there is such a person – would have had time to organise things. I'm not privy to the detail of when each guest was invited, apart from Cora of course – I asked her about a fortnight ago."

"A valid point, sir, and that's certainly something we'll have to look at carefully."

The two men sat in silence for a minute, each having much the same thought. Starling eventually put it into words.

"From what I gather in discussions over breakfast and through the morning, it seems nobody – including the heir – has any idea as to what was actually in the safe. It must be a huge problem for you, not knowing what – if anything – is missing."

"Matter of fact, it's worse than that, sir. We're not even sure if the safe was opened at all."

Starling stared at him. "But surely...?"

"Oh, we can surmise, of course," interrupted Rees. But we don't know. But you're right – we are working in the dark. I've sent a cable to the *Ile de France*, and I hope to get a reply from Lord Tallis tomorrow.

"I can't think of any more questions at the moment, Mr Starling, but something may occur to me later which I'll need to ask all of you."

Starling rose to leave, and had neared the door when he turned back to the detective. "Suppose Tallis tells you that the safe was full of jewellery, Inspector – will you be searching the house?"

Rees smiled. "If he says so, and gives a description of what is missing, then yes. At present, we can't see how anything could have been removed from the house. But we'll have to await the information from his lordship."

CHAPTER 12

After Starling had left, the DI walked up and down the room for several minutes, until a tap at the door produced a new interviewee.

"I'm Charity Carey," announced a young woman. "I must tell you this sort of thing is all new to me, and very worrying."

Rees shook her hand, and indicated an armchair. After they had both sat down, each appraised the other. It was patently evident that Mrs Carey was Patricia's younger sibling – there was perhaps a three-year age difference, but the facial resemblance was almost exact.

Before Rees could make a start with the interview, the telephone rang again, and he decided to assume the call would be for him. Rising with a word of apology, he went to the desk and picked up the instrument.

There was a gabble of words in his ear, and he told the speaker to slow down and start again. At the second attempt, Rees gathered that the caller was the Sergeant at his local police station.

"We've had a message telephoned in from a shipping company, sir, I can't pronounce the name but it's French. They said it's from the Eel for you personally. Don't know what the Eel is, but this is like a telegram."

"Just read it please, Dalby."

"Yes sir.

'No jewellery or other valuables in safe. Perhaps sixty or seventy pounds in cash. Cash book in safe will confirm exact amount. Principal content is paperwork. Twenty-one documents, most only two or three pages. Some of these of considerable but non-financial value to limited number of persons. Cannot return for at least ten days, but am arranging for code to be sent to Hammond, with instructions. Conditions. Hammond, Walter, and one senior police officer are the only ones to be in the room when the safe is opened. Documents are highly sensitive and confidential. Police officer may read any item remaining which relates to a person in the house, but I expect him to forget everything irrelevant to murder. Hammond is familiar with all documents. If one or more is missing he can identify subject or subjects. If only one item missing he can identify culprit, although proof will be more difficult. If more papers are missing, he can offer names to narrow down investigation. If no papers are missing and money intact then safe probably not opened. After check, H will take all documents and lock them in office safe, as house safe compromised. Am nearing New York; cable findings to Hay-Adams in Washington. Tallis.'

Sergeant Dalby paused. "That's it, sir. Shall I repeat it?"

"No; I've got the gist, thanks. Just leave your note on my desk."

Rees returned to his seat, and apologised again.

"That was a cable from your father, ma'am. He's being very helpful. If that had been a telegram within this country it would have been very expensive – I can't imagine what it cost ship-to-shore. Anyway, no doubt you've heard from other people what questions I've been asking, so perhaps you could answer them for me."

Mrs Carey gave a brief smile. "Yes, Inspector. First, I have no idea what father might have in the safe. I've never seen it open. I've never heard of this man Skinner before, but if he broke in believing it was full of valuables, I think his information was faulty. Given the number of items that father has given to my sisters and sister-in-law, I can't think that there's much if any of mother's jewellery left in there. I suppose there might have been some money.

Mrs Carey paused. "Now, you want to know about the embarrassing matter of the invitations. I don't know what you said to Norman, but he wasn't happy before he came to see you, and he's been like a bear with a sore head ever since. Anyway, I invited Bruce Leach. As I've no doubt you've heard, I nearly married him. For the avoidance of doubt, as the lawyers say, there has been nothing between us since I married Norman – Bruce and I have simply remained friends, whatever my husband may think."

She paused again, to see if Rees was going to

ask for more details, but he remained silent.

"It seems to have been father's intention to arrange for a disparate set of guests to stir things up in some way. God know why, as that's never been his style – thoroughly uncontroversial and even staid, I should have described him. However, although we've had this murder, of course, actually most of the invitees seem quite decent people that one can get on with. There seems to be some tensions between a few people, but nothing that's developed into a full-blown row. I admit to having an intense dislike of the Saunders woman, but I hope you'll agree that isn't unreasonable?"

The DI didn't answer this, although having met Carey, and heard about his conduct with Miss Saunders, he privately agreed with Charity.

'When did you invite Mr Leach, ma'am?"

"About ten days ago, Inspector – the day after I discovered Norman was inviting his girlfriend."

Rees thought that Mrs Carey expected him to respond to this description of Miss Saunders, but he chose to ignore it – for the present at least.

"Thank you for all that, ma'am. All these little things go into the melting pot, and eventually we hope to reach the solution to the mystery." He rose to see the latest interviewee out.

Within seconds, the hostess appeared again.

"You have my sister-in-law coming along in a minute, Inspector, but I just wanted to see if there's anything else we can get you?"

"Thank you, ma'am, I'm fine. But I do have one more question for you while you're here. Delicate, maybe, but this is a murder enquiry. The sleeping arrangements, now. Officially, or unofficially if you are aware, who is sharing a bedroom?"

The telephone rang again before the chatelaine could reply, but this time the DI ignored it, and it quickly stopped ringing.

Mrs Burgess smiled. "I was expecting the question. The answer is straightforward. All the married couples are sleeping together. I don't care to elaborate on this, but in one or two cases that may be causing some friction. To my knowledge, there has been no other movement between bedrooms, although I don't patrol the corridors all night to check."

Jill Tallis arrived in time to hear her sister-in-law's remark.

"I think that's right, Pat," she said with a laugh, "but I suspect that a day or two ago perhaps someone might have been looking forward to a wander along the corridor after lights out. Circumstances may have changed!"

Rees was left to work out for himself to whom Mrs Tallis referred, but it didn't seem an insuperable problem.

Both ladies were clearly amused by the situation, and Mrs Burgess continued the speculation.

"Ah, yes, Jill, but maybe there's one or two

new potential partnerships to make up for that one!"

They both laughed again, before looking apologetically at Rees. "Sorry, Inspector, not helpful to you," said Mrs Tallis.

"Probably not, madam, although as I've already said to one or two other people, every little snippet may be useful in this sort of enquiry. Anyway, I think I've heard enough in the last few hours to decipher what you're both saying, so I won't press you further."

Mrs Burgess left the room, and the DI invited Mrs Tallis to sit down. The first part of the ensuing conversation almost exactly duplicated that which he'd had with Charity Carey a few minutes earlier. However, when asked why she hadn't opted to invite someone herself, Jill Tallis snorted.

"I'm very fond of my father-in-law, inspector, and until he came up with this proposal I've always had the greatest respect for him. But I thought his idea was ridiculous, and that if all eight of us invited some awkward stranger, what should be a nice family celebration was likely to be ruined.

"I declined to participate, although as you know my husband exercised his option and invited Eustace Beaumont. Eustace can't by any stretch of the imagination be classed as an oddball, of course. As it happened, most of the other invitees are similarly inoffensive, and if it really was father's intention to sow dissension in the ranks I think he would have been disappointed by some of the choices if he'd been here!"

"When you say 'most' of the invitees are inoffensive…"

"Oh, you must have learned what I mean. Five of the six are middle-class people who in most circumstances could fit in anywhere. But a crooked solicitor? Emily – and I've said this to her face – should never have invited him.

"And Norman invited the absolutely appalling Cissie. While he, like Em, might have been slavishly following Edgar's wishes, it would have been a lot safer if he'd kept her hidden in his office and invited someone he'd met in the street – a taxi driver, say, or a greengrocer – instead."

"I wonder if his lordship would really have been disappointed, ma'am. If, as most of you seem to believe, he wanted to create mayhem, one could hardly do better than to have a real murder on the premises."

"That's true, I suppose," conceded Mrs Tallis, "certainly so if it turns out that one of the guests is involved."

Rees was just rising preparatory to seeing the lady out when there was a tap on the door and Walter Tallis poke his head into the room. Seeing his wife still sitting down, he muttered an apology and started to withdraw again. Rees called him back.

"Please come in, Mr Tallis; your wife and I have just about finished, and I'm guessing that you bring news."

Tallis nodded, and came across the room to sit on the arm of his wife's chair.

"May I stay to hear this news?" she enquired. Tallis looked at Rees.

"Oh yes, Mrs Tallis; no reason why not. I heard from your father-in-law a short while ago, and I anticipate that your husband has also heard from him, probably via Mr Hammond."

"Quite correct, Inspector. Meredith cabled the ship, as you evidently did. He has just called me. As I assume father has told you, there is nothing in the safe which would be of interest to an average burglar. But there are documents. Father has sent the safe combination to Meredith, who is unable to get here until half past seven tonight. I've agreed that time with him – I hope that is satisfactory. Father has issued strict instructions about the procedure – he's cabled me too, and understand he's also sent a message to you."

"Yes; only you, Hammond and I are to be in the room when the safe is opened. I don't know if he has put you under the same condition, sir, but I am to forget everything I see which has no relevance to this case! I rather think that Mr Hammond may already have some knowledge about what these papers say."

Tallis smiled grimly. "I'm sure you're right about that, Inspector. But I'm also certain that whatever these documents say, nothing in them will be to my father's detriment; it's much more likely that they hold secrets about other people. He would never blackmail anyone, of course, but knowing everything possible about someone before entering a contract with them is very sensible. I'm sure one of Meredith's jobs is to do background checks on people with whom father intended to do business. Glad I wasn't given the job – I wouldn't have known where to start!

"Anyway, we'll soon see what's inside. It occurs to me that if the safe was indeed opened before the burglar was shot, the killer may have been given or somehow acquired the combination. He could open it again later."

"Quite right, sir, and his lordship has anticipated that. Mr Hammond is to remove any remaining papers and deposit them in the office safe."

There was another knock on the door, and this time it was the head of Emily, the youngest daughter, which appeared.

"Do come in, Mrs Starling," Rees called across the room, "we've just finished."

"Don't be jealous thinking the Inspector allowed each of us to have a witness, Em," said Tallis, smiling at his sister. "The fact is that Jill was being cross-examined on her own – I just popped in at the end with some information."

"Oh, I'm not worried, Walt. I've heard various stories about these interrogations, but nobody has said Inspector Rees has been employing thumbscrews or the rack. And I don't think he's been saving me until last because he knew I have such exciting testimony to give, and wanted to wait as long as possible in anticipation. I know absolutely nothing."

Tallis and Jill Burgess both gave Emily a hug as they went out.

CHAPTER 13

"Not much point in formally introducing myself now, ma'am. Come and sit down."

The youngest Tallis sister was another almost identical copy of Patricia and Charity. While she had been standing beside her brother, the likeness to him had also been clearly discernible. No question of the late Lady Tallis having produced a cuckoo, the DI thought irreverently.

Sorry to disappoint you, ma'am," he started with a clumsy joke, "my thumbscrews are in for repair."

He patiently went through the same process as he had with all the others, and eventually came to the guests.

"I'm embarrassed," said Mrs Starling. "As you must know by now, I invited Maurice Todd. I've known him for years, and for some reason feel sorry for him. I thought he fitted in exactly with what my father seemed to want. As an ex-convict he isn't respectable – although he's served his punishment now – but he knows which knife and fork to use, and can join in any intelligent conversation. With hindsight, I suppose it was a mistake. There's never been anything between

Maurice and me, but Craig wasn't happy when I told him. So he decided to invite Cora – retaliation in a way, I think. Cora seems all right, actually, and I rather doubt if she's ever had an affair with my husband. But there we are."

"When did you issue your invitation?"

"About a fortnight ago, Inspector. Is that significant?"

"It may be, ma'am. You'll appreciate that a professional safebreaker wouldn't be available at a moment's notice. One would have to be found – probably not easy – and then commissioned to do the job. Delicate negotiations, likely. So someone who was only invited here a day or two ago wouldn't have had time to organise that."

"Yes, I see. I hear this man was a Londoner. As you say, finding someone of his, er profession, wouldn't be easy. I for one wouldn't know where to start looking!"

"What about the other guests, ma'am – had you met them all before?"

"Yes – all except Cissie Saunders. Apart from Maurice, and Jonathan Payne whom I know from the Company, I didn't know any of them well, though. Not likely any of us would have met Cissie before. She's also a Londoner, of course – any chance the murderer was a woman?"

"Quite possible – the only strength required was the ability to pull the trigger of a pistol. But presumably a great deal of mental strength.

"Another embarrassing matter, ma'am. I

believe you have given money to Mr Todd on several occasions. Is your husband aware of those gifts?"

Mrs Starling flushed. "There was no reason for Maurice to tell you that. But in answer to your question, no, Craig doesn't know. Most of the income in our household is mine, and we have separate accounts as well as a joint one. I haven't mentioned the matter at home, because Craig would almost certainly misunderstand and create a fuss. I hope he isn't going to learn about this from you?"

"Certainly not, ma'am. I've already gathered several bits of confidential information, and I expect to receive more when your father's safe is opened later tonight. None of that will ever be divulged, unless it happens to be crucial evidence in this murder case. But perhaps you'd better ensure that Mr Todd never tells your husband about his wife's generosity."

"I certainly will, assuming he hasn't been stupid enough to do so already. How are you getting into the safe? Have you found another safebreaker, or are you getting some garage man with one of those gas torch things?"

"An oxy-acetylene cutter – no, nothing so complicated. Your father is providing the code to let us get in the easy way."

Mrs Starling looked surprised, but then realised what must have happened. "Oh, Marconigrams, I should have remembered. That's how they caught Crippen, of course. Well, it'll be interesting to see what's left in the safe. We've all been speculating about what attracted this burglar in the first place. My sisters and Jill and I have been given what I think must be every last bit of mother's jewellery, so we don't believe there was any of that left even before the safe was burgled. If it was, of course," she bumbled on.

The DI thought that there was nothing further to be obtained from Mrs Starling, and rose.

"Thank you for your help, ma'am; that's all I need at present."

Rees felt very tired, even though he had had no exercise all day. He rose and stretched, before going to look out of the window, thinking he might take a turn around the house. However, although it was now dark he could see that it was snowing hard, and so abandoned his idea. The mantel clock showed the time as being twenty to seven. He had thought it was later, but on pulling out his own half-hunter found that the two timepieces concurred to the minute. He decided to relax in an armchair and close his eyes for half an hour. He found a short catnap refreshing, but rarely had the opportunity to enjoy one during a typical working day.

He managed twenty minutes sleep, and was woken by a tap on the door. This time it was Partridge.

"Mrs Burgess requires me to ask whether you would care for some hot food later, sir, if you are still here. The family and guests will dine at eight o'clock. We can serve the full meal here for you."

Rees thought about this for only a moment.

"Thank you, Partridge, and please thank Mrs Burgess for the kind offer, but I'll say 'no'. I hope to be on my way home before eight."

The Butler gave an almost imperceptible bow, and left the room. The DI sighed, and closed his eyes again.

This time he failed to lose consciousness, but spent the next ten minutes reviewing what little he had learned.

CHAPTER 14

At seven-twenty, Walter Tallis entered the study, ushering another man before him.

"Meredith, this is Detective Inspector Rees, he announced; Inspector, this is Meredith Hammond, my father's principal secretary and right-hand man."

Rees appraised Hammond as he shook hands. He saw a man of perhaps a little under average height, clean-shaven, with neatly parted 'mouse' coloured hair, dressed in an open-necked shirt, sports jacket and flannel trousers. There was nothing unusual about the man's appearance, thought the DI – yet he was immediately conscious that there was something exceptional here. 'Presence' was the word which came to mind. Perhaps it was the piercing eyes, he thought, set in this otherwise unimposing face.

To the DI's surprise, Hammond seemed to take charge. "Perhaps if we sit down for a minute, gentlemen, we can review what instructions each of us has received from Lord Tallis."

With a faint grin on his face, Walter Tallis led the way to the armchairs.

"Suppose I tell you both what my extensive orders are, continued Hammond, "and we can see if either of you has anything different.

"I have been given the combination to open the safe. Assuming that works, and I can open the door, I am to see what, if any, documents remain. As I am familiar with all of these – although I was only responsible for drawing up about half of them – I am to look through them and ascertain if any are missing.

"Walter here has told me which family members and guests are here. You, Inspector, are to be allowed to view any document relating to someone currently present in this house. You, Walt, are to be given the option to read any of the documents; it's a matter for you.

"If one or more documents are missing, I am to inform both of you to whom those papers refer, and to give you a brief summary of what they say.

"If all the documents have been taken, I am to give you the names of each person in the house who was the subject of one of these documents, Inspector.

"There may be other possible outcomes, but I suggest we cross those bridges if we reach them. Any questions?"

Both men shook their heads. "Concurs with father's cable to me," confirmed Tallis. "I'd like to defer my decision until we see which documents are left."

Hammond rose, and walked across the study to the safe. By tacit agreement, the other two men remained seated at the other end of the room, and watched.

Hammond crouched in front of the safe, and without consulting any notes began to twiddle the dial. Seconds later, he turned the big handle, and swung the heavy door open.

He twisted around to look over his shoulder. "Before I touch anything inside, are you intending to check for fingerprints, Inspector?"

"No, you carry on, sir. There were no prints on the pistol, and I hardly think the killer would have been so stupid as to remove his gloves again before fiddling around with the safe contents."

Meredith turned back to the safe. He first removed two bundles of banknotes, a black metal cash box with a key sitting in the lock, and a small book.

"I won't bother to count this now – it is clear that theft of money wasn't the object of the exercise. There's nothing else in here except this cardboard box. Let's look in that."

Hammond lifted out the box, and brought it to the desk.

Tallis and Rees looked at each other, but again stayed where they were.

Hammond sat in Lord Tallis's swivel chair, lifted out the heap of papers, and put it down in front of him. The watchers could see that the documents were in clusters, each tied with pink ribbon. He looked at the top set, smiled faintly, and returned it to the box without unfastening the ribbon. He repeated this procedure for the next twelve papers.

The fourteenth paper he put to one side. The last three also went back in the box. Bringing the little bundle with him, he came and sat down again with the others.

"Well gentlemen, this is the position – could have been better, could have been worse.

"There are definitely four documents missing. Your province, Inspector, but one could surmise that the killer took the one concerning him, together with three others – the people are also present in the house – to muddy the waters.

"This set of documents also relates to someone in the house, Todd, but my guess would be that the murderer, having got his own papers and a few red herrings, didn't bother to go any further down the pile – this one was quite near the bottom."

"That's logical, sir," said the DI. "This has certainly put us in a far better position than we were in a few minutes ago. I'm glad that last set was near the bottom – if our man had seen them I guess we'd be looking at five suspects now rather than four!"

"Man – or woman – Inspector. One of the four is a female – Cissie Saunders. The other three are Starling, Leach, and Carey."

Tallis sat up sharply. "Family? Oh dear, oh dear."

He shook his head slowly. "I had no idea father vetted people to this extent, although thinking back I think he gave me one or two hints over the years."

"I know he thought it best that for the time being at least no member of the family should be aware of any – shall we say problems – concerning any other member," replied Hammond.

"Meredith, I've decided that I don't want to read these things for myself at present. I'll talk it over with father when he returns. But just tell me one thing, please. Do the reports on Starling and Carey explain why neither has ever been offered a place on any of the boards?"

"I'm not privy to your father's thinking on that point. I did the research on those two – some of it several years ago, incidentally – and made my report. But knowing his lordship's strict adherence to his belief in honesty, professionalism, integrity, decency, and so on, I shouldn't be at all surprised if their absence from the Company is effectively a result of what I wrote."

Tallis nodded slowly. "I see. I must say that I've never seen either of them show evidence of any talent which would be useful in an executive or even a non-executive position. So I've never suggested such a thing to father.

"But I assume that your findings go rather further than simple lack of ability. Still, you two talk it over – I'll leave you to it while I go and have a think. Even without knowing the detail, I'm going to find it hard to face the two of them now. I just pray that neither is the murderer."

Left alone, Hammond and the DI looked at

each other.

Hammond pushed across to Rees the documents which he hadn't returned to the box. "Take a look at these first, Inspector, then we'll come to the missing ones."

The report on Maurice Todd was comprehensive. The first paper was dated some three years earlier, and reported, in remarkable detail, about some of Todd's dealings – including the matter for which he would later be convicted. Other potentially criminal offences of the same type were mentioned – although it would seem that these had either not yet been discovered by the authorities, or it had been decided not to pursue them in view of the first conviction and sentence. Attached to the first report was an addendum, dated earlier in the current month. This merely mentioned what Rees already knew – that Emily Starling had been making payments to Todd. This report remarked that while some payments had been made by cheque, it was believed that others had been made in cash.

Rees looked up. "I see that you sign this report, and presumably wrote it. But surely you must have agents or the like to do the actual digging?"

Hammond smiled. "Oh yes, a small army of informants. Some of them, as you'll realise later, in very high positions. And although all of the information comes to me for collating, as it were, and I can find out a great deal through my own contacts, some of it is gathered by Edgar Tallis himself. I really don't know how. Perhaps he calls in favours; perhaps he pulls rank. If he wants to find out about someone, he will be able to do it somehow. You'll hear about an example of his power in a minute."

The DI pushed the papers back to Hammond, and sat silently for a minute.

"If Todd's papers had been missing, the motive would have been plain – the wish to suppress damaging documents," he said at last. "Presumably what you're about to tell me about the other four will be similar?"

"In two cases, certainly; perhaps in three. But with respect, Inspector, it may be premature to assume that the murderer is one of the four. It's just possible that he or she thought the correct papers had been grabbed, but made a mistake – perhaps there wasn't enough light to see properly. Or – and I agree this is even more unlikely – that taking the documents was a red herring, and for some reason it was simply necessary to eliminate the safebreaker, perhaps because he knew of some other secret regarding the killer. This might have been a way to get the burglar into a compromising situation, and simultaneously produce a few suspects."

Rees considered this for a few seconds. "I can't buy either of those theories, sir. I don't even want to think about them – the complexity would drive me mad. Just tell me about the four missing documents, please."

"Yes, of course. The report on Cissie Saunders is the most recent of the three, and the most straightforward. Nothing criminal; just a report on her intimate male friendships. Not to put too fine a point on it, she provides sexual favours for money. What is sometimes called a 'high-class prostitute'. She's not a streetwalker, certainly. Carey has had intimate relations with her – there are details of hotel assignations and so on. Statements by hotel staff, too. Whether that was part of her job, as it were, or whether he paid separately, we didn't determine.

"Incidentally, of the five people we're considering, I think Miss Saunders is the only one who probably doesn't know she has been investigated."

Next is Leach. But these documents aren't actually about the Honourable Bruce. He only gets a brief mention – respectable war service, no criminal record, nothing else known to his detriment. Not very popular in either his regiment or his club, but that's hardly an indication that he might be a murderer.

"No, the papers relate to his father Angus, 1st Baron Leach of Culgower in the county of Sutherland. One of the very few people I've ever met that I should describe as unrelievedly obnoxious.

"Leach runs a similar sort of empire to Edgar's, although they aren't direct competitors.

Similar upper middle-class backgrounds, but the senior Leach doesn't possess a single one of Edgar's many positive attributes. Leach is a bully and a crook – a really nasty piece of work. The documents provide evidence to show that three major Government contracts were obtained through a mixture of fraud and bribery. Those are effectively sample cases – there are certainly other instances. But when I reported on these three, Edgar said it wasn't worth spending time and money looking further. I had also uncovered a case where a company prospectus had been issued with known falsehoods included. Also a criminal offence, of course.

"However, Edgar told me he was investigating something else – and set me working on the same matter, albeit at a more modest level. He said he knew for a fact that Leach had bought his title. Such things have always gone on, no doubt, but of course it's now common knowledge that the instances became particularly egregious after the war.

"This is an example of the power my boss exerts. He had found three people, all at very high level, who had been involved in Leach's ennobling. God know how he did it, but about fourteen years ago he obtained formal affidavits from each of the three. What they had done wasn't illegal at the time, so I suppose they had little to lose. They're all dead now anyway. If they did today what they did then, each would be guilty of an offence under the

1925 Act, and get up to two years inside.

"My more recent task, about eighteen months ago, was to provide additional evidence of the payment. That wasn't hard to find – bank employees aren't remunerated well. In fact Angus Leach paid forty-five thousand pounds via a single cheque, and two further sums – twenty and twenty-five thousand pounds in cash."

He paused, and raised his eyebrows. "Got all that, Inspector?"

"Oh yes, sir. I suppose I'm not really surprised at goings-on of this sort, but hearing about them does leave a nasty taste in the mouth. Please go on."

"Now we come to the sons in law. Carey first. Adultery may be contrary to the seventh Commandment, but it isn't a criminal offence in this country. If it were, Carey would be guilty many times over. He has actually had a paternity order made against him – about a month ago. I'm not quite sure whether Charity is aware of that – she is certainly aware that he hasn't been faithful. I'll make an awful pun here – given that his business barely shows a profit, he'll be even more reliant on Charity to make the paternity payments.

"I know the lady, of course – she does a good job as a non-exec in one of our companies. She isn't afraid to speak out. My gut feeling is that she won't be afraid to divorce her husband if the final straw comes along. A costly procedure, of course, but she can afford it – and I don't doubt that her father would support her anyway.

"But Carey isn't at risk of going to prison for anything?"

"Not unless he's committed for non-payment," replied Hammond. He isn't a criminal like Todd, or the elder Leach, or – as I'll explain next – Starling.

Starling runs three companies. One is an import-export business. It was that which drew him into contact with Edgar Tallis. Four or five years ago, we used Starling's firm to import some materials, when another supplier failed. Had Edgar known then what we subsequently discovered about Starling, he would never have put business his way.

"All three firms are, not to put too fine a point on it, built on sand. A crooked accountant helps Starling to juggle the figures, robbing Peter to pay Paul, trying to keep the creditors happy. I won't go into detail, but Starling is guilty of several offences – varieties of false accounting, forgery, and so on. If this becomes public, he's looking at a minimum of two years as an involuntary guest of His Majesty, and probably nearer five.

"And I can tell you that they certainly will become public within the next few weeks, whether or not you charge him as part of your current investigation."

Rees gave Hammond a puzzled look. "Even if I was included to pursue something disconnected with the murder, the evidence against Starling has gone now."

Hammond leaned back in his chair, and smiled. "Actually, it hasn't disappeared," he said. My very lengthy cable from Edgar instructs me to tell you two other things.

"First, all the key documents that were in this safe have been duplicated. Some photographically, others just with transcripts. But all have been stamped by a Commissioner for Oaths as being true and correct copies of the originals. And the three key Leach affidavits aren't just copies – Edgar got all three men to sign two identical affidavits at the same time. So we still have originals of those.

"I was aware of the duplicates, but have never known where they are kept – safely in a bank vault somewhere, I expect. One assumes that Edgar anticipated, right from the start, the possibility of someone getting access to his safe!"

The DI had visibly brightened. "That's very good news," he remarked, although we still have too many suspects. What's the other thing?"

"My instructions are very clear. On request, I am to provide the police with any assistance within my power. Edgar is very unhappy that this murder has happened in his home. Money is no object. I wondered if, perhaps, it would be helpful if I set people to investigate this safebreaker – see if we could find out who he came into contact with during the past few weeks, that sort of thing."

Rees smiled for almost the first time that

day. "That might well be very helpful, sir. Extremely generous of his lordship."

"Yes. I'll initiate that tomorrow. Just ask if you want anything else done. We'll do nothing to embarrass the police, of course, although we may need to use methods which the police cannot.

"There's something else. I am instructed to make it very clear to you that my help is unconditional. Specifically, I am to do nothing to shield either Carey or Starling – their stones can be lifted for you to see what lies underneath, just as for the other suspects."

The DI nodded slowly. "Not a lot of love lost there, then. Although with good reason, evidently. I wonder if he has spoken to the two daughters to warn them about their husbands."

"Not yet, I think. However, I believe he intends to do so as soon as he returns. As I said a minute ago, Starling's peccadilloes will get to the ear of the authorities very soon – I'm just awaiting the instruction to give them the evidence – and I'm sure he'll want to tell Emily what is to happen before her husband is arrested. I don't know if Charity is to be told about Craig, but I think it probable."

"Hmm. When talking to the two ladies, I didn't get the impression that either thought her husband was a knight in shining white armour. Ah well."

"I think you're right in that. I'm not staying overnight, Inspector. I even declined an invitation to dinner. Some of these people already know I've been digging into their personal lives. When you start questioning them again tomorrow, I'm sure my name will be mud. I could do without metaphorical daggers being thrown at me across the drawing room or the dinner table. Walter tells me that the relationships out there aren't wholly amicable already!

"I don't know how you intend to play this tomorrow, and it isn't my business, of course. But one piece of advice, if I may. It might be sensible not to say anything about the duplicate documents to start with. Perhaps hold on to that until you've had a talk with the four leading runners – and then spring it on them."

"I appreciate any advice you can give me, sir," replied the DI. "I'll be very frank, although I wouldn't like you to quote me. I don't have your education or your intelligence, and I don't have the police experience in murder cases to make up for that lack. So I'm delighted to receive any advice you may care to give me. Also, I don't even have a second-in-command with whom I can have a discussion, so I'd appreciate being able to talk to you about things over the next few days."

Hammond smiled. "Of course. Call me at any time. Take my card, so you have my private number as well as the office one -and I'll tell my staff that you are to be put through to me immediately, whatever I'm doing."

"Will you report to Lord Tallis on what has

been found, sir? That would save the cost to the public purse of another cablegram from me!"

"Yes, Inspector, I'll bring him up to date in the morning."

He rose to go. "I'd like to go home too, sir," said Rees. 'But now we know what's missing, I'm going to have to carry out a quick search of the relevant bedrooms. Mrs Burgess has already agreed to a search without the need for a warrant. Complete waste of time, of course – I expect the papers went on the fire within minutes."

Hammond considered whether or not to suggest that a general grant of consent from the chatelaine might not constitute consent from individuals for a search of their personal effects, but in the end decided to say nothing. He pressed the button to call for someone, and within half a minute a maid arrived.

"Ah, Trixie, please inform Mr Tallis and Mrs Burgess that I'm leaving," said Hammond. "They'll no doubt be at dinner, so I'll just slip away without ceremony."

"I also need you to show me to a number of bedrooms," added Rees.

The girl, knowing Hammond's profession, and his standing with Lord Tallis, looked at him almost enquiringly. Hammond gave her a firm nod.

He replaced the cash box and the treasury notes in the safe, closed and locked the door, and spun the dial. He added Todd's documents to the remaining papers in the box, picked it up, and all three moved to the door. "I'll get these in the office safe tonight," he remarked. "Seems unlikely you'll need them, but just say if you do."

CHAPTER 15

The next morning, Sergeant Knowles arrived at the police station at a few minutes before eight. He found his boss already seated at his desk, staring morosely into space. From experience, Knowles knew better than to interrupt with even a 'good morning'. He sat at his own desk, and started to write the report of his findings in London.

Ten minutes passed, and Rees stirred. He seemed to notice his assistant for the first time. "Right Sergeant, let me fill you in on what's happened here."

The DI spend the next twenty minutes giving his number two the details of the previous day's events. He didn't tell Knowles about the help to be provided from Hammond. The Sergeant didn't interrupt to ask any questions, and the only indication he gave that he was actually taking in what he was being told was that his eyebrows rose a couple of times. The last item concerned the DI's search.

"I spent an hour and a half looking through the five bedrooms rooms while everyone was at dinner. No sign of any papers, but then I never expected to find them."

When Rees eventually came to the end of

the briefing, there was silence. The DI knew that his Sergeant was now processing the information he had been given. It was an unfortunate fact, Rees thought, that however less intelligent he himself was than someone like Meredith Hammond, the fact was that Knowles was significantly still further down the scale. After two clear minutes of thought, Knowles spoke.

"One of the sons-in-law, then, sir? The crook or the womaniser?"

"Possibly. But it could still be any of the four whose papers are missing. Or the bent solicitor, Todd, even though his papers are still there. Or a third party that we don't know about."

Rees mentioned Hammond's alternatives, but Knowles, after mulling these over, said he didn't believe either theory. The DI took little interest in his Sergeant's opinions, and probably wouldn't have commented even if he hadn't agreed with this one anyway.

"Today, I want you to interview all the indoor servants, from the Butler down. I don't seriously suspect any of them of the murder, but they may know something. In particular, ask each person if they heard anything during the night – the shot probably wasn't heard outside the study, but perhaps someone heard movement afterwards – a bedroom door closing, or something of that sort. But also ask for comments about these four people – and better include Todd too. The servants may be reluctant to talk about the family, but you must emphasise that this is a murder enquiry, and blind loyalty isn't appropriate. Gossip isn't evidence, but it is often indicative of something useful. Get the idea?

"One more thing. Pound to a penny the documents have been destroyed, almost certainly by burning them. I expected to find fires in the bedrooms, but although there are fireplaces it's clear they haven't been used for years. Radiators and things, now. So where else might someone burn evidence?"

"I expect there's a range or something in the kitchen, sir."

"There is, yes; I've seen it. But there must also be some sort of boiler for the new heating system. So we need to check for fingerprints around both kitchen and boiler room. On doors and door handles, on the doors where you put coke or coal in, on pokers, anything. Dust everything you can see. Should have done this yesterday, but better late than never.

"Assuming you get some prints, take exclusion prints from the servants. See what, if anything, isn't accounted for."

Knowles confirmed that he understood what his boss wanted.

Rees made a conscious decision to avoid his Superintendent, telling himself that he had nothing of significance to report anyway. The two detectives left the police station, and travelled in the same car to Wythall. Partridge opened the front door himself. If he felt that the detectives should have gone round to the rear, he didn't say so.

"Good morning, Mr Partridge. Two things, if you please. First, Sergeant Knowles here is going to look for fingerprints around the fires in the kitchen and boiler room or whatever you have to heat the pipes.

When he's done that, he is to interview you and all your house staff. Obviously he will try to do that with as little disruption as possible to your no doubt busy schedules, but each interview shouldn't take more than five or so minutes. Perhaps you will find a suitable room, and arrange the best time for each person to see him."

The Butler gave one of his imperceptible bows. "That will be arranged, Inspector. If the Sergeant cares to come with me now, we can get started."

"The other thing, Mr Partridge, is that perhaps you will inform either Mrs Burgess or Mr Tallis that I'd appreciate a brief word in the study as soon as convenient."

The Butler gave a marginally deeper bow, and stalked off down the corridor with Knowles carrying the fingerprint kitbag at his heels. The DI smiled to himself, and continued to the study. There he drew back the curtains and stood for a moment looking out at the gardens. He then sat down, still gazing outside. His reverie was quickly interrupted, as Walter Tallis entered the room, and sat down in another armchair.

"'Morning, Inspector. How did your chat with Meredith go last night?"

"We found nothing that points the finger unambiguously at a particular person, I'm sorry to say, sir. But useful – yes, I think I can safely say that. Certain information that limits the number of possible killers, and almost if not completely eliminates others. For your ears only, if you please, sir, that group includes you, your sisters, your wife, and Mr Burgess."

"Very pleased to hear that, Inspector. Hardly surprised, though. What do you want to do this morning?"

"I'd appreciate a short meeting with all the family and guests together. "I want to make a short statement, and then I'll be interviewing those whose documents are – or were – in the safe, and who therefore aren't quite so much in the clear as the others.

"While I'm doing that, Sergeant Knowles is interviewing the staff. I apologise for setting that up before speaking to Mrs Burgess, but Partridge has it all in hand."

"No problem, Inspector. I'll inform Patricia now. Give me ten minutes, and I'll get everyone ready for you. The dining room will be best, I think. I'll come and fetch you when I have everyone corralled."

Once again left to himself, Rees returned to his reverie. It took rather longer than Tallis had expected to collect everyone together, and it was nearly thirty minutes later when he returned with an apology.

"Couldn't find Charity, and couldn't find Cissie either. Ran my sister down eventually, in a bathroom. Between you and me, she was crying. Husband problem, I gather, but we didn't have time to discuss it. She's okay to join us. Found Cissie in the servants' hall, of all places, talking to Cook. If you're ready, come along."

The DI followed Tallis along the hall, and they turned into the big dining room. The rectangular table was bare, apart from two silver centrepieces. It could have seated at least twenty people with ease, thought Rees, as he came into the room. Tallis indicated to Rees that he should take the carver chair at one end of the table, and took a seat himself a couple of places down, next to Cora McBride.

"Good morning, ladies and gentlemen," began the DI. "I'm sorry to disrupt your morning, but I won't keep you here for many minutes. Over the rest of the morning, I'm going to be interviewing some of you again, and rather than having to explain what's been happening several times, I thought it would be easier to say it to all of you in a group.

"Before I start, I should tell you that I have received a lengthy cable from Lord Tallis in mid-Atlantic. Mr Tallis here has also heard from his father. His lordship's Principal Secretary, Mr

Hammond, who is known to most of you, has received another – the longest.

"What I'm going to say now will be a surprise to some of you – but alas not to all.

"The safebreaker did succeed in opening the safe. We know from Lord Tallis what it contained. There was no jewellery, and only a modest amount of cash. Incidentally, the burglar – or the person who killed him – left the money untouched. The only things of value in the safe were documents – each of which would be of value to only one or at most two people. That value might be enormous – although not measured financially.

"Last night, we opened the safe again, Lord Tallis having provided the combination. We know exactly how many documents were in the safe. And we now know which ones have been removed. Fortunately, we also know what the missing ones said."

Rees, who had been speaking without notes and running his eyes continuously around the seated men and women, paused.

"Speaking as one who is surprised, Inspector," said Cora, "I don't even understand what these valuable documents are."

"You are indeed on my list of those who would be surprised, Mrs McBride. The documents are private reports on various different people, some of whom are present in this room. These reports include sworn statements – affidavits if you like – together in some cases with official certificates and so on." He paused again. This time Cornelius Burgess spoke.

"Can one assume that these reports are not exactly flattering about their subjects, Inspector?"

"That would be one way of putting it, sir. Another way would be to say that they are damning. It doesn't take a Sherlock Holmes to deduce that person who killed the safebreaker is very probably one of those whose embarrassing documents are now missing."

There was a short silence. Rees noted that although the siblings had exchanged some glances, none of the four main 'document holders' (as he thought of them) looked anywhere but down at the table. The fifth, Cissie Saunders, just stared at him.

"Do you expect me to be surprised, Inspector? Because I certainly am!"

"I thought you would be surprised, Miss Saunders, although I have to tell you that there is indeed a short report about you."

Cissie glared, first at him, and then at Norman Carey. "Did you know about this?" she shouted.

"I knew people had been looking into me, but I had no idea that they'd investigated you," he replied, sharply. "Be quiet now, and listen."

"Just a minute," Cissie continued, still clearly upset. "Tell me this – is it the police been snooping on me? They got no right."

The DI was about to reply, when Walter

Tallis stirred. "No, my dear," he said. "The Inspector will correct me if I'm wrong, but I think the police knew nothing about these papers until last night. The investigations were carried out by my father, or at least on his instructions. Right, Inspector?"

There was dead silence around the table. "Quite correct, sir," replied Rees.

"Something I don't understand," said Charity. "How do you know what is in the reports which have gone missing?"

"A very good question, Mrs Carey," replied Rees. He looked across to see if Tallis was going to intervene again. After a faint nod from the DI, Tallis answered the question.

"The fact is that Meredith produced – or at least collated – these reports on father's behalf, and his memory is such that he can probably quote verbatim from any of these documents."

There was a short silence. This was broken by Payne, with a somewhat sardonic smile on his face. "You seem a bit reluctant to name the remaining characters, Inspector. I too am surprised. Am I in the same category as Cissie?"

"Oh no, Mr Payne. The four other people I shall be interviewing again are well aware of the existence of these reports, although they may not all realise the full extent of them. The four are Messrs Todd, Starling, Carey, and Leach.

"I'll only have one or two more general questions for the rest of you."

The DI could see that all the others were looking at the five named people. None of the looks appeared sympathetic, perhaps with the exception of Emily's towards Todd.

Leach was scowling. "You allege that I am one of those investigated, Inspector. But I am as surprised as Miss Saunders. Not only was I unaware that I have been spied on, but I'm sure my life has been pretty much blameless."

"I suggest you wait until I talk to you separately, sir; all will be explained then.

"Now, come along to the study, please Miss Saunders; I don't expect to keep you very long."

Rees stood up, and the girl reluctantly followed him out of the room. After they left, the others slowly rose, and silently dispersed. The four siblings, plus Jill, Cornelius, Eustace, Jonathan and Cora, moved to the drawing room. By tacit agreement, none of the other four joined them, and each went up to his room.

In the drawing room, after a few minutes' desultory conversation, Jonathan Payne realised that the presence in the room of Cora, Beaumont and himself was a constraint on the family having a private discussion, and tactfully suggested that he and the others should withdraw. There were a few polite "no, no, my dear chap," remarks, but what Payne had said was so evidently correct that without further ado the three stood up and left the room. Beaumont said he would go outside for some fresh air, and Payne led Cora along the hall

PETER ZANDER-HOWELL

into the library.

CHAPTER 16

"Take a seat," Rees told Cissie when they reached the study. The girl was now very subdued.

"This isn't very nice," she said. "But whatever it says in that report, I haven't killed anyone. What does it say about me, anyway?"

"None of this is very nice, Miss. I don't suppose Mr Skinner thought it was nice for someone to shoot him. The report on you was, I understand, incidental to the report on Mr Carey. However, it contradicts what you told me about your relationship not going beyond a kiss and a cuddle in the office. It gives clear details of various assignations with him – dates, name of the hotel, witness statements from staff members."

"Oh, hell," said the girl. "But nobody could think I'd organise someone to destroy that."

"I'm inclined to agree. But you should know that there were details of more assignations, with other men. And evidence of payments received."

Cissie flushed. "Just being a prostitute isn't illegal."

"No; and in fact, I still don't seriously suspect you of murder. But you may have some information to help me. Yesterday, you said that Mr Carey didn't seem to like Lord Tallis. Do you know why not?"

Cissie shook her head. "I've only known Norman for a few months. Yes, he was one of my clients, and later he gave me a job in his office – to 'reform' me, I suppose. But almost from the first I heard him make nasty remarks about his lordship. Two or three times he moaned that he wasn't given a directorship when he married the daughter. But maybe some of the hostility was because he knew he'd been spied on and caught out going with me."

"Yes, perhaps. I shouldn't say this, but as I understand it's all going to come out now anyway, you may as well know that you were not the only woman Mr Carey was unfaithful with."

"I can't say as I'm surprised, Inspector. How else can I help?"

"Delicate question, Miss. The night before last, did Mr Carey come to your room?"

Cissie gave a hollow laugh. "You must be joking. As I told you before, he's barely spoke to me since we arrived. Anyway, I doubt if he could've sneaked out of his room without his wife knowing."

"Did you hear anyone else moving around during the night – say between midnight and three o'clock?"

"Sorry, no."

"All right, Miss Saunders. I guess you probably don't want to stay in this house any longer than you need to. So you're free to leave. If

Mr Burgess is still happy to drive you to the station, please tell him that he can do that as long as he comes straight back."

"Thanks." When Cissie got to the door, she turned. "How long will it be before everyone learns what I've been?"

"Possibly never. The police have no reason to publish any details about you, and we won't be doing so. I have a feeling that Lord Tallis has no interest in humiliating you either – although he may not feel the same about one or two others. The risk for you is if Mr Carey's wife files for divorce. If she can't get sufficient evidence somewhere else I suppose she might cite you."

Nodding sadly, Cissie disappeared. A few moments later, Mrs Burgess looked around the door, left ajar by the departing girl.

"I've ordered some coffee and biscuits for you, Inspector, and I've also arranged some for your Sergeant. If you say who your next candidate is to be, I'll go and find him."

Very kind, Mrs Burgess, thank you. It doesn't really matter – whichever one of the gentlemen you see first.

"But just before you go, I have one question. The night before last – did you hear anyone moving around after midnight?"

"Alas, no. The rooms in this house were designed, I suspect, to be almost soundproof. In any case, both Cornelius and I are heavy sleepers.

"By the way, you can probably imagine

what's going on around the house. Craig and Norman seem to be hiding away in their bedrooms, each man keeping out of the way of his wife's wrath. The rest of the family members are in the drawing room. My sisters are in a real tizzy, wondering what the reports say about their husbands, and which of them might be the murderer. The other three are tactfully keeping out of the way.

"Within these walls, Inspector, I've never understood what my sisters saw in their respective husbands. I shouldn't really admit to this, but if my brothers-in-law get some sort of comeuppance, I'll get a certain tinge of pleasure. There's no appropriate word for that in English, but the Germans call it *schadenfreude*. Anyway, I'll see who I can find."

Rees had never heard the word, but correctly deduced its meaning.

Patricia left the room, almost colliding with a maid carrying a tray.

"Put it down on the little table by the armchairs, Lizzie," she instructed.

"Thank you, Lizzie," said the DI when the mistress had gone. "You had a horrible shock yesterday, I'm afraid. I hope you're feeling better now?"

"Yes, sir, thank you sir. Mrs Hobbs said as I was to bring your coffee myself now. She reckoned I've got to come in here again sometime, and best to get it over with."

"She's right, Lizzie. Me, I've never been on a horse, but 'tis said that if you fall off one, best get back on as soon as possible."

The maid giggled, but as she turned to leave noticed the tarpaulin still covering the bloodstains, and the smile left her face again. Giving a quick curtsey, she almost ran out.

Rees had just poured some coffee, and sat down again in his armchair, when a tap on the door preceded the entry of Norman Carey. To say that Carey looked unhappy would have been a serious understatement. Rees invited him to sit.

"Can't offer you coffee," he said; "they've only brought one cup."

Carey shook his head impatiently. "Just get on with it, please. I'm sure you've heard a lot of stuff about me from Hammond, and no doubt Cissie has told you a good bit more. Yes, I plead guilty to being a philanderer. An adulterer, in fact. But I've broken no law, and I'm certainly not a murderer!"

"Someone is, Mr Carey. Have you told your wife that you have a paternity order against you?"

Carey looked down at the floor. "Oh God. No," he admitted.

"I gather the income from your business is minimal, and you are reliant on your wife's money to stay afloat. Is that correct?"

"Why ask if you already know?"

"So, you expect your wife to stump up not only for this child, but also for your visits to prostitutes?"

Carey was silent, still apparently gazing at his shoes.

"Well, I think it is crystal clear that you have a very strong motive for suppressing that report."

"I suppose I can't deny that. But the hoo-hah resulting from this incident will probably lead to Charity divorcing me. I'd have been better off if no burglary had occurred, and very possibly Tallis would have continued to keep silent. He's certainly kept quiet about it for months already – I realised over a year ago that enquiries were being made."

"That's a fair point. I shall have to think about it."

"But there's something else, Inspector. Even if I'd have found this burglar and arranged things – which I didn't – why should I kill the man? Once he's opened the safe, why not just collect my papers, pay him off, and let him go again?"

"Another fair point. But that applies to the others too. Whether it was you or someone else, I think the answer has to be that the murderer didn't want a single living witness. Perhaps the safebreaker was stupid enough to read the documents before handing them over – who knows?"

The DI fixed his gaze on Carey. "I said in the dining room earlier that some documents are missing, but others aren't. You haven't asked which category yours are in. Is that because you already know they're missing?"

"No, it certainly isn't. I hadn't really thought about the difference. As far as my own position is concerned, it doesn't matter either way – whichever it is, the information about me is coming out."

Rees grunted. "All right. Your report was among the missing papers. Of the five people concerned that I mentioned earlier, the papers on only one remained in the safe. What, if anything, we can deduce from that remains to be seen.

"Now, although you still remain on the list of suspects, I don't see any reason to keep you here any longer. Would you prefer to leave?"

"To be honest, I'm not sure what's best. But I have to talk things through with Charity sometime. Better try to get that done here, I think. So I'll stay for a while – unless Pat decides to throw me out of the house immediately."

"Can I go and find you another candidate, Inspector?"

"Thank you; yes please. Doesn't matter who, really – Todd, Leach, or Starling."

CHAPTER 17

The DI was just finishing his second cup of coffee when he was joined by Sergeant Knowles, who announced that he had finished his task.

I've seen thirteen people, sir, from Partridge down to the boot boy. I never realised before how important rank is in a place like this – there are three different levels of maid here, for instance, and each is required to know her place.

"Anyway, nobody heard a thing the other night. But they all sleep well away from the posh bedrooms, and not even on the same floor.

"Only interesting thing was that several people – including the Butler, when I'd persuaded him that loyalty and discretion aren't applicable in a murder case – told me what they thought of some of the people.

"They all seem to love the family, and Mr Burgess and Mrs Tallis are included. Not Messrs Starling and Carey though – half a dozen people almost spat when they were mentioned. Nobody could really explain to me why they were out of favour – someone mentioned how rude they are to the servants, but perhaps they don't tip when they're expected to."

"Or maybe the servants can sense the innate

flaws in their characters when their equals either can't or choose to turn a blind eye," replied Rees. "That wouldn't surprise me, actually. What about the popularity of the other visitors?"

"Quite funny, really. Poor Miss Saunders is looked down upon. She shouldn't be on this side of the baize door, it seems – ideas above her station! Beaumont and Payne are approved of. Todd's time inside seems to be known about in the servants' hall, and he's looked down on because – as the Housekeeper put it – 'he's not the sort of man who should be a guest in his lordship's house'. Mrs McBride was approved of, although not all the staff had met her. Nobody said much about Leach at all."

"What about prints?"

"Pretty hopeless, sir. There is a boiler room – you go down some steps from a door in the scullery. The fire door handle obviously gets very hot, so there's a big piece of rag beside the boiler which – the lad told me – is to hold the handle when you put more coke in. The handle itself is shiny clean – wiped with the rag several times a day, of course. I dusted the poker, but not even partial prints on that. There's a huge range in the kitchen which uses coal, sir. Again, people use either gloves or a cloth to open the fire door. Nothing there.

"There are two doors between this side of the house and the servants' bit. Both are sort of covered with green material like a billiards table – no chance of prints. There is a handle each side, but it's all fancy twisted brass and there's not enough of a flat surface to take a print. Anyway, both doors have those double hinges – people passing through from either direction can just push against it without touching the handle at all. There's a glass panel in them so you can see if someone is coming the other way. I watched some of the staff going through. People sort of walk into the door and push it with their body, if they're carrying something. Otherwise they push the edge of the door. The door between the kitchen and what they call the scullery has the same double-hinged arrangement. Again, the handle is useless, but the wood isn't covered with baize. That's our best hope, really – I got some reasonable prints off both sides of that. The door down to the boiler house is an ordinary door; there are some prints, but not very good ones.

"I've not taken anyone's prints for elimination as yet, sir."

"Right. We'll leave that job until later. I've seen Miss Saunders and Mr Carey. No admissions, obviously, and nothing new. Carey, who appreciates he's going to be in deep trouble with his wife, has gone to find someone else for me to see. You stay now and take notes – sit at the desk.

Two minutes later, there was a sharp knock on the door, and Bruce Leach came into the room. The DI first introduced his Sergeant, then indicated an armchair, and the three men sat down, Knowles at the desk. Leach looked enquiringly at the detective.

"In the dining room earlier, you had a question, Mr Leach. It's true that the relevant report isn't principally about you – although you were looked at. The bulk of it concerns your father. I think you are perfectly aware of that. He certainly is, and I can't believe that he hasn't discussed the matter with you, his son and heir.

"So what if he did?"

"So it would mean you have a motive. Destroying the papers would protect your father, first from a lengthy prison sentence, and secondly from it being publicly known that he bought his title. And that latter point would also apply to you – when you eventually take your seat in the Lords I don't suppose you would like people staring and sniggering."

Leach was silent for a moment. "I see," he said at last. "Well, I make no admissions about anything my father may or may not have done. But now there is no evidence against him for the alleged bribery, and probably not for any other matter either. No proof. Certainly if the police – or anyone – makes such allegations in public, my father will sue and get enormous damages."

"Why do you suppose there is no evidence, Mr Leach?"

"Because you told us the papers had gone."

"No, I did not. I said that some had gone, and that some remained. But you knew that those relating to your father had gone, didn't you? Because you removed them."

Leach looked furious. "You're trying to trap me! I must have misunderstood what you said.

"Anyway, you've now confirmed that ours are missing, so what I said remains correct. No evidence."

"It's quite true that yours have gone – and almost certainly have been totally destroyed. But you're wrong about there being no evidence."

"How so? Again without admission, I know about the people who gave statements to Tallis years ago. I also know that all three are now safely in their graves, and can't say anything more."

"Ah well, there's some things you are obviously unaware of. Much more recently, enquiries were made about money transfers from your father's account at the relevant time. There is very good evidence about the bribes. Apart from drawing out two enormous sums in cash – which just happen to correspond to the amounts paid to two of those facilitating the purchase of his title – he was foolish enough to pay the third bribe by cheque.

"That purchase was, at the time legal. But then there's the matter of his criminal activities. Much of the documentation does indeed date back some years, and I accept that it might now be difficult or even impossible to acquire fresh statements.

"However, that won't be necessary."

Rees beamed at Leach, who scowled back at him.

"You see Lord Tallis took precautions for the safekeeping of all these documents. There are duplicates – properly authenticated – of everything that was in the safe.

"Even better, the three affidavits you clearly know about were themselves created twice – each of the signatories signed two original copies on the same day. The second versions are held securely in a place where – even if you can find another safebreaker – you won't be able to reach them."

Leach sat glaring, and the two detectives later agreed that he had been grinding his teeth. "You're as good as accusing me of murder," he snarled. "If you suggest any such thing outside this room I'll have the coat off your back; and father will sue your police force and take every penny you personally possess too."

"I've been threatened many times before, Mr Leach. That sort of thing doesn't bother me. Where did you find Mr Skinner?" he added casually.

"Right – that's it," shouted Leach, standing up, "I'm going to consult a solicitor."

"Very wise, sir," returned the DI. "Perhaps you and your father could share the same one – I don't suppose there'll be a conflict of interest."

Leach turned back as he neared the door. "What are you doing about father's case? Are you going to publicise this business of his peerage?"

"Oh no, Mr Leach. That's not a police matter. But I rather think that Lord Tallis may talk to people about that quite soon. He's extremely annoyed that someone has not only violated his hospitality by arranging for a burglary, but has actually murdered someone in his home.

"The police will certainly be looking into the other allegations, though. If convicted, I understand your father is looking at five or more years inside. Of course, he's entitled to be tried before the House of Lords rather than in the county Assizes, but I imagine their lordships will be quite impartial. In any case, from what I've heard I doubt if he could count on many friends in a jury of his peers. Please don't leave the house, Mr Leach."

The man almost ran out of the door, not bothering to close it behind him.

Knowles got up and closed it. "You seem pretty confident, sir – is there enough to prove he did it?"

"No, Sergeant, there isn't. It could still just as easily be Carey, or Starling, or even Todd. I've really stuck my neck out here, by accusing Leach. But I'm gambling on the fact that when Lord Tallis starts his likely attack, and we or some of our colleagues start probing into these criminal matters, neither the father nor the son will have time to sue me! In the meantime, we'll see what else we can find.

"Go and see if you can find Starling or Todd – get a maid or someone to search if you can't see one of them quickly."

Knowles returned five minutes later. "Couldn't find either of them, sir. But in a library I saw a man and woman. The man said he wasn't Starling or Todd, and told me his name is Payne. Anyway, he rang the bell, and when a footman appeared Mr Payne instructed him to find Mr Todd and tell him to report to the study immediately. The woman was introduced as Mrs McBride, sir. I assume neither of them are suspects?"

"No, I don't think so. If I was a bookie I'd make Starling and Leach joint favourites at three-to-one on, Carey at three-to-one against, Todd at twenty-to-one, and the Saunders girl a hundred-to-one outsider. Two hundred to one bar."

The Sergeant smiled. "Never knew you were a racing man, sir. I went to the races once at Pitchcroft – saw the lines of bookies there. They were calling the odds just like you – except you aren't doing the funny tic-tac signals! I couldn't afford to place bets, and without that I found the racing boring – never went again."

"I go sometimes. But I agree with you about the betting. Deciding which nags to bet on and then placing the bets takes up most of the time. Each race only lasts a minute or two, of course – and like you I wouldn't have any interest in watching if I didn't have something resting on the result! I rarely come away from a meeting more than a pound to the good, and I'm often down on the day – but I always have a good time."

Further discussion was halted by the entry of Mrs Burgess, once again carrying out her duties as hostess, coming to enquire what the officers would like for lunch. Once again, Rees opted for "some more of your Cook's excellent sandwiches, if you please, ma'am." Knowles, who hadn't yet had a chance to sample food in the house followed his boss's lead.

Mrs Burgess had been gone for only a minute when Maurice Todd came into the study, looking even more wary than he had the day before.

"Come in, Mr Todd. You haven't met my assistant before – this is Detective Sergeant Knowles. Knowles, this is Mr Maurice Todd. Let's sit down."

Once again, Rees and Todd sat in the armchairs. Knowles, readying his notebook and pencil, remained at the big desk.

"Since we spoke yesterday, Mr Todd, have you had any further thoughts about this matter?"

"Many thoughts, Inspector, but I've come to nothing which might approach a conclusion. You've obviously been told about the report on me. I can probably guess what it said – none of it good.

"All I can say – in mitigation rather than a defence – is that having served my time I have truly learned my lesson, and will never be tempted to stray again. What I'll do I really don't know, but I won't be breaking any more laws."

Rees looked at the man for a moment in silence. "As a matter of fact, I haven't been told what was in your report – I was able to actually read it for myself. Earlier, I told you all that some of the reports on people currently in this house had been stolen, and some remained. In fact, of the five reports yours was the sole survivor."

Todd sat absorbing this information. "I see. Surely that exonerates me from this murder, then?"

"Not necessarily, Mr Todd. Consider this hypothesis. While in prison you met and had some reason to kill the man Skinner. You lure him here on the pretext of getting into the safe and stealing jewels. You shoot him. You are aware of these reports, and remove a few to cast the blame onto others. You deliberately leave your own report there. What about that for a possibility?"

"You certainly have a vivid imagination, Inspector, but your hypothesis is ridiculous. Yesterday, you asked if I served my time in London, and I said no. I guess that means that Skinner is a Londoner who has probably done time in a London prison. I'm prepared to bet that he was never in Winson Green, so I couldn't have met him there. And my crime was so-called 'white-collar' – prior to my conviction I never consorted with burglars, men of violence, sex offenders, or anyone of a criminal bent. Nor have I consorted with people like that after getting out. Good luck to you in trying to prove a motive."

"I concede that there are others who are more likely candidates than you, Mr Todd. I'm just saying that you aren't exonerated just yet.

"Your report, by the way, details offences other that the one for which you were sentenced. "I don't have time to look into those now, but colleagues will probably investigate sometime."

"I have nothing to worry about there, Inspector. I don't know when the report is dated, but I made full admissions when I was first arrested. All the other matters were dealt with as 'TICs', and although I was only charged with the single matter the Judge took the others into consideration when passing sentence. I can't now be prosecuted for them.

"Leaving aside your amusing theory, if my report had been one of those taken my point would have been that I had no reason to suppress it."

"I can't argue with that, Mr Todd. Very well; you may leave the house now, if you so wish."

Todd gave a wan smile. "Thank you. However, while I remain at least to some extent *persona grata*, I guess I'll stay for a bit. The exchanges between the various parties seems likely to get even more entertaining over the next few hours."

CHAPTER 18

"What did you make of him, Sergeant?" asked the DI. He didn't usually ask Knowles for an opinion, but this case was of unprecedented importance, and Rees was sufficiently desperate to break his habit.

"Well, sir, I admit I've never seen a murderer face to face, but he doesn't look like one to me. And he made some good points."

The detectives were interrupted by the arrival of two maids bearing trays with food and beverages. The girls fussed around setting out cups, saucers, and plates, and were just about to withdraw when Rees set another task.

"Please find Mr Starling, Trixie. Present my compliments, and inform him that I'd appreciate his presence here in the study at half past one."

Trixie acknowledged the instruction, and she and her colleague each bobbed a curtsey and left the room. The two detectives attacked the pile of sandwiches with gusto.

"Can't help hoping we have to stay here a bit longer, sir – these sandwiches are to die for."

"Yes; well, someone had to die to let us eat them! I have to agree with what you say about Todd. I'll lengthen his odds." He mimicked the arcane motions of an on-course bookmaker.

Knowles grinned. The two men carried on a desultory conversation about a concurrent case, while enjoying the simple but excellent fare provided by the chatelaine.

***

Craig Starling arrived almost on the dot of one-thirty. He too was introduced to the Sergeant.

The three sat down, and Rees and Starling looked at each other. The DI didn't appear to be in any hurry to start the interview, and Starling – already evidently nervous when he came into the room – began to fidget in his chair. A full two minutes passed, before Starling gave in.

"All right, Inspector; the silent psychological treatment has superseded the old police brutality, I see. Just tell me the worst. What does Hammond say about the report on me?"

"Earlier, Mr Starling, I told you all that some of the relevant reports were missing from the safe, and some were still present. I wonder how you know that your report is one of those missing. Presumably you know because it was you who removed it."

"No, no, I didn't," Starling replied in a sort of squeal. "I suppose I just assumed. You can't read anything into that."

"We'll have to see. Your assumption is correct, though – of the five reports on people here today, four, including yours, are missing.

"Going back to your question, the report on you makes a number of allegations. Considerable detail is given. I am informed that there is ample evidence to convict you of at least three criminal offences, all attracting custodial penalties even for first offenders. Those matters will certainly be investigated in the very near future – unless of course you are convicted of murder."

"Not me. It really wasn't. How can I make you believe me?"

"Well, in fairness to you, it's for me to prove that you did it, rather than for you to prove your innocence. And I have a bit more work to do on that as yet.

"But you admit you were aware of this report, and what it contained?"

"I can't deny knowing that private investigators were looking into my affairs, and I could surmise what they probably found. But I'd be stupid to find a burglar to steal the papers, and completely insane to kill the man."

"I can't quibble with your choice of 'stupid' and 'insane', Mr Starling. Yet it seems someone did hire a burglar, and did shoot him after he'd done what was required.

"I asked you yesterday who your money was on, but you didn't come up with an answer. Since then the field, as it were, has been reduced. As I told you earlier, the four missing reports relate to you, Miss Saunders, and Messrs Leach and Carey – and the only other relevant report is on Mr Todd.

Would you now care to offer a suggestion?"

Starling shook his head slowly. "If Todd's papers are still in the safe, he would seem to be in the clear. Surely not Cissie Saunders – this must have required a good bit of organising and she doesn't seem very bright. And I repeat, it wasn't me."

"I see – so your money's on Leach or your own brother-in-law. Well, let me tell you that you are joint favourite as far as I'm concerned."

"Now my papers have gone – presumably destroyed – can I hope that the police will forget about my other matters?"

"Oh no, Mr Starling. You are under the same misapprehension as one or two others. Although the documents which were in the safe are, as you say, probably destroyed, it seems Lord Tallis took the precaution of having certified copies made. And those are in a safer place. Quite apart from this murder, you can look forward to being charged with various counts of larceny.

"What's the atmosphere like among the family and guests at the moment?"

"I have no idea. I've avoided everyone since you spoke to us all earlier. But I imagine it's pretty poisonous. Emily and I weren't on very good terms before this, but now she knows about this report God knows what she'll be doing. And when she learns what it says, well, I'm as good as dead. I don't know what the others have been accused of, but whatever Norman's done I guess Charity won't be very forgiving. And it's a pound to a penny that the rest of the family will support Charity and Em. Oh, God.

"Todd and Leach aren't married, but if you're still keeping them here I don't think they'll be very popular in the drawing room either – not that they were universally popular before."

He paused, and looked straight at Rees. "I'm making no admissions about any other matters. But I didn't hire a burglar, and I didn't shoot him."

"We'll work flat out now to prove that one of you did. All right, Mr Starling, that's all for now."

Wordlessly, and looking far more aged than he had the day before, Starling almost crawled out of the room.

When the door closed, Knowles enquired whether his boss was adjusting the odds again.

"Yes, but only to shorten them on Leach and Starling. Did I say three-to-one on for them? It'll have to be ten-to-one on now – and in fact I think I'm closing my book as far as those two are concerned!"

"Now, there's some basic police work to be done. Trouble is, it's mostly down in London. It seems very unlikely that our man had a tame safebreaker already in his pocket, as it were. He probably made enquiries in pubs and the like, as to where a likely person could be found. We need a witness who can say that one of our suspects asked about or made contact with Skinner in the last month or so. Several witnesses, if possible."

"By heck, sir, that's a mammoth task. Even if you just took all the pubs with say a mile of Skinner's home, I guess it'd probably mean at least twenty different premises. Maybe a lot more. And it would need more than a single visit to each one to talk to enough people who might have seen our man. We don't have the manpower for this sort of exercise, and surely the Met wouldn't do that sort of extensive search for a county force?"

"All very true, Sergeant. Just the same, we'll have to show willing. However, we may have some unexpected help, although whether it'll be sufficient I don't know."

The DI explained Lord Tallis's instructions, and Hammond's offer.

Knowles looked unconvinced. "Big task for amateurs, I should have thought."

"Perhaps. I rather think some of these helpers will be professional private eyes, though – not amateurs. And I believe some of these agencies employ ex-police officers. So perhaps they know a thing or two.

"Certainly the reports on our suspects here were very thorough. We'll have to see.

"But we can't leave everything to Mr Hammond to sort out. I'll speak to the Super in a minute, and see if he's prepared to get the Chief Constable to ask the Met to lend us a couple of CID men to make some enquiries. Failing that, you and I will have to spend a few days around Camden, drinking."

"Don't mind the drinking, sir, but I hate going to 'the smoke'. I avoid the place like the plague."

The telephone rang; Rees opted to pick up the instrument – chances were the call was for someone else, but it would give him a reason to wander around looking for the right person – and perhaps to get an idea of the atmosphere elsewhere in the house. However, he found the call was indeed for him.

"Hammond here, Inspector. Can you talk?"

"Hello, sir; yes, there's only my Sergeant in the room with me."

"Right – I just thought I'd see how you're doing, and update you regarding my bit of digging. I assume your search found no papers?"

"No, nothing."

"Well, hardly surprising. Now you've probably found this out for yourself, but they don't have fires in bedrooms at Wythall anymore. Very rarely in the downstairs rooms either, except at Christmas. So I reckon the things were fed into either the kitchen range or the boiler furnace."

"Yes; we've been looking to find fingerprints on doors and so on around those two items."

"Oh, good – glad to hear you're ahead of me! Now, I have commissioned three private agencies to start sniffing around finding out everything possible about Skinner. The best is a little firm run by an ex-inspector from Scotland Yard, who has proved very capable in the past. His team will be concentrating on public houses around Camden. They'll be starting in a little while – as soon as opening time arrives."

"That's good to hear; thanks for that, sir. Going back to the possible destruction of these papers. Would you think that any of our suspects would ever normally go into or through the kitchen, and so might know where the boiler and so on is located?"

"Very unlikely, Inspector. Can't think of any reason for them to even go into the kitchen. If you want something to eat or drink, you ring the bell. However, I don't see that as relevant. These are intelligent people. They would know that there must be a big solid-fuel kitchen range. And they would know that the house is fitted with an extensive radiator system, so they would know that there must be a boiler.

"I've stayed in the house many times, and I've never been in the kitchen. But I've walked all around the outside, and I know that there is no separate building which could house a boiler. From which I surmise that the furnace is actually inside the main house – and the only logical access to that must be via the kitchen. Anyone else could work it out the same way.

"Late last night I sent a cable to Edgar Tallis, explaining what we found – and didn't find – in the safe. Within an hour I had another lengthy reply. Basically, he's hopping mad. I am to spare no expense in giving the police whatever help is required. I can tell you – this isn't to be passed on yet – that regardless of who committed the murder, he will be moving against various people as soon as he returns.

"He's probably in Washington by now, and he says he will fulfil his mission very quickly, then cut his visit short and only stay there for one night. He's aiming to get back to New York in time to sail back on the same vessel he went out on."

"I hope nobody is listening in to this call, sir," said Rees.

"Doesn't really matter, Inspector. It's unlikely to be one of the suspects, but if it is it won't do him any good to know that Edgar intends to destroy him. Although I suppose it would give him time to flee the country!"

Rees smiled to himself. "Just one point about that, sir." He explained what Todd had said about offences taken into consideration.

"Fair enough; he's probably telling the truth, although we'll double-check. Very well, I'll leave you to it. As soon as I hear anything from our people in London, I'll let you know."

Rees replaced the earpiece, and relayed to Knowles what Hammond had said.

"Let's hope these agents find something, sir. And I can't feel very sorry for any of these people that his lordship might take down!"

"Agreed. Look, Knowles, something else is worrying me. I have my favourite two suspects, as you know. But think about this. If it's Leach, he could creep back upstairs and go to bed, no problem. But if it's Starling, surely his wife would know he'd been out?"

"See what you mean, sir. Will you shift the odds again?"

"May have to, I suppose. Pity; I'd almost decided on Starling. Still, we'll see. Right, you go away and persuade all the staff to let you take their prints. Then see what, if anything, remains unaccounted for."

Left on his own again, the DI picked up the telephone. However, it was already in use, and he listened for a moment to an innocuous conversation which he soon gathered was between the Housekeeper and an errant butcher. He replaced the earpiece. Five minutes later, he tried again, and found the line was now clear.

The operator, after some confusion, connected him to his police station, where after more delay he was eventually able to speak to Superintendent Foster.

Rees gave his report, uninterrupted by his superior. At the end, the DI asked if the Met. could be persuaded to provide a little help.

"I don't know, Rees," said Foster. "On the one hand I'm uneasy about these private people trying to do police work – even if some of them are ex-coppers. On the other hand, I don't know that the Met would just lend us some men for something like this. And they'd charge us quite a bit too, I imagine. Anyway, I've never been involved, but I think if a county force asks the Yard for help, they come along and run the whole show, rather than just lending people. But I'll talk to the Chief, and see what he says."

Five minutes later, the study telephone rang again, and once again Rees picked up the instrument. The Superintendent was on the line, sounding surprised.

"The Chief Constable is on his way to Wythall to see you, Rees – I've no idea why. So stay put. And mind your Ps and Qs when you talk to him!"

The DI rarely saw his ultimate boss, and had spoken with him perhaps five times in as many years. Sighing at the thought of even more pressure likely to be put on him, Rees got up and pressed the bell push. To his surprise, a minute later Walter Tallis arrived.

"Sorry, Inspector; Pettit was on his way here to answer the bell. Thought I'd come instead and see what you need."

"I was only going to ask him to inform you and Mrs Burgess that Colonel Meadows, the Chief Constable, will be arriving here shortly to have a discussion with me."

"Oh, I know Meadows quite well. He's one of father's friends. I'll tell Pat he's coming, although I assume his visit is not in any way a social call and he won't want to meet the family. I'll instruct Partridge to show him straight in here, and get you both some tea. If he would like to speak with anyone else, just ring.

"I suppose you can't tell me how your investigations are going?"

"Not as well as I'd like, sir. You heard me mention five names this morning. Although I can't definitely eliminate anyone, it looks as though Mr Todd and Miss Saunders are in the clear. And, of course, it's still remotely possible that it wasn't one of the three at all."

"Oh dear; my brothers-in-law are still 'in the frame', then. Charity and Emily are in deep discussions with Pat. Beats me what they have to discuss, actually, as nobody has all the facts. Anyway, Jill, Cornelius and I are keeping out of it for the moment – but I expect to be dragged in at some point," he added gloomily.

"I'm working on the possibility that the documents were burned in the boiler furnace or the kitchen grate," said Rees. "As you may see if you go anywhere near the kitchen, my Sergeant is engaged in looking for fingerprints on doors and so on."

Tallis considered this. "Yes, that does seem a likely way of getting rid of the papers. Certainly too risky to hang on to them."

Shaking his head, Tallis left the room. Rees sat back to think. Half an hour later, he was no further forward. Hearing the distant jangle of the front door bell, he stood up and brushed himself down with his hands, anticipating the arrival of his boss.

CHAPTER 19

At the front door, Partridge welcomed Colonel Meadows, a frequent visitor to the house.

"Good afternoon, sir. Mr Walter anticipates that you won't want to speak to members of the family under these circumstances, so I am instructed to take you straight through to the study to see your Inspector. May I take your coat and hat?"

"Quite correct, Partridge. No, I'll shed the coat in the study. When we've finished, I'll just let myself out again without disturbing you. Against protocol, I know, but these are unusual circumstances."

"Indeed, sir," replied the Butler, as he escorted the Chief Constable across the hall towards the study. "Refreshments will be brought in five minutes, sir," he added as he knocked on the door and opened it for the visitor.

The DI stood rigidly to attention as Meadows entered the room.

"Stand easy, Rees, and in fact let's sit down in comfort." Colonel Meadows tossed his hat onto the table, and hung his coat on the back of a chair. The two men moved over to the armchairs. "Now, Mr Foster has told me very little; only that you want to ask Scotland Yard for some help up in London. Forget that for a minute, and give me an outline of the case from the beginning."

Marshalling his thoughts quickly, the DI gave the CC the basic facts, and what had been discovered so far.

Meadows sat silently for a minute. Before he could speak again, the Butler arrived, escorting two of the maids with trays. When the tea had been poured, and the staff gone again, Meadows looked at the DI.

"Good summary, Rees. A sad affair for the family. For this man Skinner too, of course, although we can't waste much sympathy on him. Not sure if it's a good thing Tallis isn't here, or not.

"So let me recap. Tell me if I'm going wrong. Sounds like your favourite is young Leach. I've met him, but can't take to him at all. Motive really is as proxy for his father, who's at risk of prison. But the son himself might be embarrassed on coming into the title if people know it was bought. On the other hand, the titles of half of the peers have less-than honourable origins. Is buying a title for cash in the 20th century any more shameful than acquiring one in the 17th century simply because you were born on the wrong side of the blanket and your father just happened to be the king?

"Your next choice is Starling. I often visit this house, but have never met the man – although Emily has been here without him sometimes. You think he is slightly less likely than Leach because he'd have had to creep back to bed with his wife and she'd probably notice. Still, he certainly has a clear motive for removing documents.

"Carey and Todd seem to be lower down your list. While a guest here I've never met Carey either. I've heard of Todd, of course, although as you know it was Birmingham CID that nabbed him. The Saunders woman doesn't seem to have a motive at all, really.

"You accept that there's a remote possibility of somebody other than those five being responsible, but that would seem to imply that the killing was a personal matter between Skinner and the murderer, and that the documents were irrelevant. I can't buy that idea at all.

"So, how to narrow the field. You seem to be pinning your hopes on finding a print which would show that one of the suspects went through into the servants' domain. Worth trying, of course. But while I've been staying here, I've gone along to the kitchen myself a couple of times – to thank Cook, that sort of thing. A print in the boiler room might be harder for someone to explain, but one on the doors in the corridor – well, that might add a bit of circumstantial evidence, but it wouldn't be nearly enough to convince a jury. In fact, if that, plus being one of several whose embarrassing papers were stolen, is all we had, the judge wouldn't let it go to the jury at all.

"Now – let's come to the request you put to Superintendent Foster. This is really why I've come.

"I've spoken to the Yard – the Assistant Commissioner (Crime). He pointed out that there are probably fifty public houses within easy walking distance of Skinner's home. It would take several visits to each one, on different days and at different times, to have any chance of finding a link. And that's assuming our killer found Skinner via a pub connection anyway. No way can the Yard find the manpower for that sort of operation – even if we could afford to pay them to do it.

"We have to abandon that idea. Now, you say Tallis has instructed his people to help the police in any possible way. I've known young Hammond all his life – he's my godson, matter of fact. His father and I were commissioned on the same day in 1900. I only made half-colonel, but Harry – about the most intelligent man I ever met – has gone on to reach Lieutenant General, and he's still serving. But according to him young Meredith is much brighter than he is. You must make every possible use of him.

"You say he suggested using private eyes to look at the pub connections. Good – encourage him. But also, don't be afraid to discuss things with him. Within these four walls, he'll be a damn sight better at thinking than your Sergeant."

Rees, aware of his own capacity, thought sadly that his own brain, though certainly more effective than that of Knowles, must rank in a far lower league than Hammond's.

"Anyway," continued Meadows, "Hammond won't betray your confidence, and may come up with some good ideas – and probably provide funds from Tallis to back them up if necessary. You follow?"

"Yes sir. I must say he impressed me from the start. Actually, I like his lordship's son and daughters, and two of their partners, and I've opened up a bit to Mr Tallis already. But it's difficult with them because, even if they're innocent, the possibility that another family member could be guilty makes one wary – they might try to muddy the waters to protect someone."

"Very unlikely, in my opinion," said the Chief Constable. "For a couple of years or so I've had a feeling that Messrs Starling and Carey are merely tolerated, not loved and respected. But you're right to be cautious, of course. Do you know when Lord Tallis will get back?"

"Not exactly, sir. In his cable to me he didn't say, but in a more recent one to Mr Hammond he said he was cutting his Washington stay to only one night, and would come home as soon as he could get back to New York. If he sails on the *Ile de France* again, I can find out when she's due to dock, but I think it'll be at least four days before he could get here."

"Mmm. You say Hammond implied that Lord Tallis is likely to see that Starling is prosecuted?"

"I'm pretty sure that's what he meant, sir."

"Yes. Well, If Edgar takes on Starling, I can't think he'll ignore Carey, even if that idiot hasn't broken the law. Work coming up for at least one divorce lawyer, I'm thinking.

"Right; I'm not helping by sitting here. I've explained what's what about the London end. You encourage young Hammond, although I suspect he won't need much pushing. I'm off." He picked up his hat and coat.

Rees accompanied his superior to the entrance hall, where Partridge mysteriously appeared to open the front door.

"Mrs Burgess presents her compliments, sir, and wishes to inform you that she hopes you will be able to return in the near future, when things are back to normal."

"Indeed, Partridge, I hope so too; thank you."

***

The DI returned to the study, where he sat almost immobile for ten minutes and only came out of his reverie when Sergeant Knowles joined him.

"Heard the Chief has been and gone, sir. Assumed he wouldn't want to see me, even if he knew I was here, so I kept away."

"Yes; the only news is that we can't get any help from the Yard. We're on our own, with whatever Mr Hammond can provide. What have you got?"

"No problem with the staff. Eliminating them, there are only two unidentified prints. One is on the scullery door, and the other – identical – on the boiler house door. Neither is what you'd call very good, but if we found a match there are just about sufficient points to use them in evidence."

"I see. I could do with moving around a bit. Take me along to the kitchen, and show me these doors."

Knowles led the Inspector into the corridor leading to the servants' empire. As they passed through the two baize-covered doors, Rees saw what his subordinate meant.

In the huge kitchen, Rees again thanked the Cook effusively for the various superb sandwiches he had enjoyed, and Knowles added his own thanks. It was clear that the woman appreciated the praise.

The Sergeant showed his superior the door to the scullery, and through that they went through another door and descended some steps into a boiler room. Here, beside a furnace, was a large pile of coke, which was clearly delivered via a hatch in the ceiling. The Inspector eyed these arrangements for a minute. A further door was set into another wall, and Rees indicated this with his thumb. "Where does that go?" he enquired.

"Out into the garden, sir."

The DI grunted, and led the way back up to the kitchen.

"This range, Mrs Green – is it always alight?"

"During the day, always; winter and summer alike. I can tell you it gets mighty hot in here in the summer. At six o'clock every morning, the lad clears out the ashes and so on, and lights the fire. It burns all day 'til about half past nine, when we let it die down. Enough heat to make our cocoa just before bedtime."

"So would the fire be out by, say, midnight?"

"I doubt it, Inspector. Low, but probably still alight. But it's pretty well cold by the time Percy comes to start it up next day."

"What about the boiler furnace?"

"I have nowt to do with that. But I think it gets stoked up last thing at night, and then Percy does whatever's necessary the next morning. Don't think it's ever allowed to really die down this time of year."

"Last question, Mrs Green. The outside door in the boiler house. Do you know who uses that?"

"Well, I know of two. Percy, of course, when he carts the ashes and so on out of here and out of the boiler. And John Carmichael, the head gardener. When he comes to see his lordship, he always comes and goes that way – it's convenient for him, I suppose, the boiler house door being close by his greenhouses."

The DI thanked the woman again, and returned to the study with Knowles.

"Better find this man Carmichael, Sergeant. Pound to a penny his are the prints you found. I never expected any success with the exercise anyway."

He sat for a moment, staring at the

temporary repair to the window pane. Returning to earth, he reached over and pressed the bell push. "I think I'd like to talk to the two wives," he told his sergeant.

The bell produced a uniformed footman. "Who are you?" enquired the DI, who hadn't seen the man before.

"This is Mason, sir," said Knowles, quickly.

"Right, Mason; please see if you can find either Mrs Starling or Mrs Carey, and ask whoever you see first if she could spare me five minutes."

The footman bowed, and left without speaking.

"You go and look for this gardener, Sergeant. If those prints are indeed his, that's another dead end."

Within two minutes, Charity arrived. Rees, mentally thinking for a word to describe her appearance, settled on 'stressed'. He fussed around her, and got her seated.

"I really am sorry to have to subject you to this, Mrs Carey, but I have to ask a couple of questions."

"Oh, I quite understand, Inspector. You don't have to worry about upsetting me. Nothing you ask me, or indeed say, is going to make my present condition any worse!"

"I suppose not, madam. Well, first of all, has your husband explained what the documents relating to him reveal?"

"Since you spoke to us all this morning,

we've hardly spoken. We exchanged a few words just before lunch, when I asked a direct question about the report on him. He said the time wasn't right to discuss it. He didn't join us for lunch. Perhaps unsurprisingly, Craig didn't come down either, although both Bruce and Maurice were sufficiently thick-skinned to do so. As a result, the meal was eaten in almost total silence. And I gather Cissie Saunders has left the house, with your consent.

"But although Norman hasn't deigned to put me in the picture, I have a pretty good idea what the report will say. He's a philanderer. I imagine it will show a number of liaisons with females of one sort or another. The Saunders woman is, I guess, only one example. That he thought it appropriate to flaunt her here, in my presence, must tell you something of his respect for me.

"Will you expand on that, Inspector, or must it remain hidden from me?"

"I don't think I can give you the details yet, madam. However, I rather think that you will learn about them when your father returns, even if your husband doesn't tell you earlier."

"I see. You had a second question?"

"Yes. Please remember now that I am not implying that your husband is guilty of murder – I'm simply trying to see how various people might have been able to do it. You told me before that your husband seemed to have cooled towards Miss Saunders, and would therefore have been unlikely to have gone off to visit her room on the night in question. But my question is this. If he had left the room, for that or any other purpose, and returned later, would you have noticed?"

Charity's face broke into a rather cruel smile. "In normal circumstances, the answer would be 'yes'. I am a light sleeper. But the morning after the incident, I woke much later than usual, and felt very strange. I had also had an unbroken night. Looking back, I am pretty certain that Norman slipped me something – is it called a Mickey Finn? – much earlier in the evening, probably when he brought me a drink at some point.

"I think something occurred between him and Cissie that evening which precluded his visiting her later, but that was probably after he had fixed me. So, although I doubt if he went to her room, I can't say that he couldn't have slipped back into bed after killing the burglar. A terrible thing for a wife to say, but I'm not going to lie for him."

The detective and the wife looked at each other for some time without speaking.

"I see; thank you for that, Mrs Carey. I really do sympathise with your position. I wonder if you would see if your sister, Mrs Starling, could spare me a minute now?"

Charity nodded, and rose. Rees went to the door and opened it for her. "I can hardly stop you telling your sister what I'm going to ask," he remarked, "but it really doesn't matter."

Emily came into the room a few minutes

later. She looked to be in a similar state to her sister, but managed a smile. When she was seated, she opened the conversation.

"Well, Inspector, what a sorry situation. Sad for the man Skinner, of course, but for some or the rest of us too, in a different way. Charity has told you of her belief that she was drugged. That doesn't apply to me – but it wouldn't have been necessary in my case. I sleep like the proverbial log. I gather Craig often gets up in the night, but I never hear him do so. Once I'm off to sleep, that's it until morning. So, if he went down to shoot this burglar, and then returned to bed afterwards, I'd be none the wiser. And Craig would be well aware of the fact.

"In answer to your other question, no – my husband refuses to discuss the content of the report on him. He says he'll talk about it in a day or two, when he's 'had time to think about what's best'. By which, I'm quite sure, he mean's what's best for him.

"I assume you won't put me out of my misery and tell me what the report says?"

"I don't think it's within my remit, madam. But, as I've just said to your sister, I rather think that your father will give you that information, if your husband doesn't. Anyway, thank you for being frank.

Mrs Starling left the room, and Rees returned to his contemplation of the window. A few minutes later Mrs Burgess arrived again.

"My goodness, Inspector, you really are setting the cat among the pigeons," she remarked with a broad smile. My sisters were fairly negative about their spouses before they came to see you, but now they are positively spitting.

"Anyway, I'm here again in my hostess capacity. Can I have food brought for you and your Sergeant, if he is still here?"

Rees considered the offer. "Very kind, madam," he said at last. "But I think we'll be leaving you in peace very shortly, so I'll say thank you, but no. I can't say when we'll be back – various enquiries are in train, and it may be a few days. So there are no further restrictions on movements in and out of the house; perhaps you will convey that to everyone."

"Of course, Inspector. I hope you find the man responsible soon, though. It's a curious situation for those of us in the family who have been exonerated, still knowing that there is a good chance that another family member might be a murderer. My sisters are especially concerned, of course – but I suppose that won't change much even if neither of their husbands is guilty of murder."

"We'll do our best to solve this, madam," replied the DI and Mrs Burgess went out of the room and Sergeant Knowles entered.

"Dead end, sir, I'm afraid." reported Knowles. "The gardener's prints without doubt."

"As expected. Ah well, let's go back to the

station."

In the car, Rees gave his sergeant the gist of what the two sisters had said about the sleeping patterns.

"So it still could have been either of the in-laws."

"Yes; although Starling seems to have a stronger motive. But we have no proof whatsoever. I do wonder what caused the alleged spat between Cissie and Carey. Can't have just been his wife's displeasure – he must have anticipated that before bringing her."

A mile or so further on, Rees spoke again, almost to himself. "I hate this situation, having to rely on unknown and untested helpers."

CHAPTER 20

There were no developments the next day, although Hammond telephoned the police station to confirm that his agents were hard at work. Rees passed on the information that the sisters had given him, and the two men had a short but inconclusive discussion. The following day, Hammond called again.

"A bit of news, Inspector, although not enough as yet to let you arrest anyone! It seems that Carey may be guilty of more than philandering. We've uncovered an illegal scheme involving bribery. I'm told there will soon be sufficient information to allow a prosecution. The incident happened prior to the earlier report, so I'm annoyed that it wasn't uncovered then. Point is this, though. Carey, knowing people were investigating, might have expected this matter to have been found. All I'm saying at this stage is that he probably has as good a motive now as Starling."

Rees thanked his informant, and after some further chat, hung up. Nothing further happened over the following weekend, and on the Monday morning Superintendent Foster was making acid remarks about the lack of progress. However, in the afternoon Hammond called Rees again.

"Movement at last," he reported. "It seems that Skinner's probable recruiter was Cissie Saunders, so you may need to rethink your theories. She certainly knew the man since childhood. Her family, and his, lived very close together in Peckham. Several members of both families had – and still have – criminal tendencies. Her own father has several convictions for burglary himself. It's impossible to believe that she wouldn't have known about Danny Skinner's specialism. Will you bring her in?"

"Yes, I think so, given it's our only gleam of light at present, and the Superintendent is on my back. Well, this would seem to confirm that our killer is Carey. So if he did drug his wife, it wasn't to go visiting another bedroom but to cover his return after dealing with Skinner. Anyway, when we've got her here, I'll keep you informed as to what she says. Many thanks for your work, of course."

Rees quickly gave Knowles the gist of what Hammond had said. "Tomorrow morning, take a constable, and get down to London. Car or train, I don't mind. Find Miss Saunders, who may or may not still be working for Carey. Arrest her on suspicion of murder, caution her, and bring her back here. Don't discuss anything about the case while she's in your custody, but make a note of anything she says. I'll contact the relevant Met division to tell them you're in their patch. Better be ready to stay overnight, in case you can't find her

DEATH OF A SAFEBREAKER

tomorrow at work or at the address she gave us.

"Oh, and if you find her at Carey's office, and bump into him, say nothing about his own possible involvement."

Rees went home that evening happier than he had been for a week. He felt sure that Cissie Saunders, faced with a charge of either murder or of being an accessory before the fact (which in law amounted to much the same thing), would soon talk.

The next morning, he walked along the corridor to the Superintendent's room, and gave his boss an update. He had hardly sat down again at his own desk when his telephone rang.

"Hammond here again, Inspector. Two things, really. First, we now have all the pieces necessary to get a conviction against Carey. That's a matter for the Met police, and I imagine the information will reach them fairly soon.

"But the second point is that Lord Tallis is back in the country. He'll arrive home late this evening, and would appreciate a visit from you and me tomorrow afternoon. Is that okay?"

"Yes, of course. It's down to his largesse and your help that we're making any progress in this murder. Shall I come at about 3 o'clock?"

"Assume that time is suitable, unless I contact you again. Presumably you'll have interviewed the Saunders woman by then."

"Yes, unless my officers aren't able to find her today."

"Good; then provisionally I'll see you tomorrow at Wythall."

A few minutes after one o'clock, just as Rees was about to put down his pen and go in search of some lunch, the telephone rang again.

"Knowles here, sir. We picked Saunders up, no trouble. She was at Carey's office. She's very fidgety, as you might expect. I'd say frightened, actually. Keeps saying she knows nothing about this murder, but Bryant and me, we aren't replying. She also mentioned she's expecting to be given notice very soon.

"Carey wasn't about, so no problem there. We're at Euston now, getting an express to New Street. We've got a car at the station, so we should be back with you soon after five o'clock."

At six-fifteen, Rees and Knowles had Miss Saunders brought into an interview room. Seated across the table from the two detectives, she had evidently been crying.

"Not a nice thing to do, Cissie, to shoot your dad's old friend. You'll hang for that. How much did Norman pay you to hire Danny for the job?"

"No, no, no; I didn't shoot him – you got it all wrong!" The girl dissolved into floods of tears again.

"You'd better tell us your version of events, then. But at the moment, it looks very clear to me – and it's a jury you'll have to convince, not just us. Speak slowly, so the Sergeant can take it all down."

CHAPTER 21

The following afternoon, Rees drove slowly out to Wythall. As he went along, he was considering what tasks remained to be completed before the case could be presented in court. However, these were now sufficiently straightforward to allow him to spend some time singing to himself. The DI's tenor voice was, as he himself recognised, never going to attract anything other than a volley of rotten tomatoes should he go on stage and sing to an audience. He didn't even sing in his bath, as other men often do, for fear a neighbour would hear and make adverse comments. However, in the total privacy of his car, he was in the habit of exercising his lungs, particularly when things were going well. Although not possessing a drop of Scottish blood, one of his favourite singers was Sir Larry Lauder. He now belted out *A Wee Deoch an' Doris*, and followed this up with *Keep Right On To The End Of The Road*. For a change, he then switched to Cole Porter, and was well into *Anything Goes* when he stopped the car in front of the big house.

Rees was surprised when the front door was opened before he had even reached the topmost step, and he was greeted by Walter Tallis, who must have been looking out for him.

"Good afternoon, Inspector," said Tallis. "Give your coat and hat to Pettit here, and we'll go along and meet my father."

Tallis led the way to the study, a room the DI now knew very well. He wondered if the temporary repair to the French window had now been made permanent, but a quick glance as he entered the room only showed the heavy curtains closed against the unpleasant weather outside.

The two men sitting in the armchairs rose as he entered. The older came forward, hand extended.

"I'm Edgar Tallis, Inspector, welcome back to my home. You've met Hammond, of course. Take a pew. Have your ordered tea, Walter?"

His son nodded, and indicated to Rees and Hammond that they should sit with his father in the comfortable armchairs. He then pulled the desk chair across to join the group, and sat on that.

"We'll wait for the refreshments before we get down to business, gentlemen," announced Lord Tallis. I confess to being very tired. I don't find trans-Atlantic crossings at all restful. I've been across seven or eight times, but this was the first time I'd travelled with CGT, and actually the first time I didn't keep thinking about icebergs!

"When I arrived in America, I had to dash down to Washington, rush around meeting people, and – thanks to what happened here – dash back to New York again. I'm getting too old for all that."

Rees observed both Walter Tallis and Hammond grinning at each other.

"Call me sycophantic if you like," said the latter, "but I bet everyone on the ship who didn't know you, thought you were a man twenty years younger than you are."

"Quite right," confirmed the younger Tallis. "And my guess is that you travelled on a French ship so very few passengers would know your real age and comment on your youthful behaviour!"

"What rot!" Tallis responded, but he was laughing, and the DI noted that he didn't refute his son's theory. "I've been across in several White Star ships, notably the Majestic – which used to be the German liner Bismarck – and also the Olympic, Titanic's sister. And the Cunard ship, Aquitania, before the merger with White Star. Now, all of those vessels feature a lot of French in their cuisine – all very well for those who like that sort of thing, I suppose. But one could always ask for something more basic. That's the only complaint I have about the CGT ships – they are run superbly, without doubt – but at the dining table it's no use asking for an English dish," he added with a broad grin.

His three listeners all burst into laughter at this self-denigrating picture of a Francophobe English 'milord'. Rees and Hammond, although totally different in every way, were both wondering exactly the same thing – what on earth did the waiters on the French ship make of Lord

Tallis?

Rees also had another thought. If he himself were rich enough to travel in this way, what would he do faced with an exclusively French menu? Perhaps if one travelled second or third class, he thought, the cuisine might be more to his taste. Or did the lower orders in France also eat snails and frogs legs? Rees hurriedly put this thought aside as Tallis started describing the remarkable railway stations he had passed through. "Architecturally, Penn station is, in its way, as beautiful as almost any cathedral in the world. If you ever go to New York, you must visit the Grand Central station too. Aesthetically just as worthwhile as the Statue of Liberty or the Empire State Building. We have some very decent railway architecture in Britain, of course, but nothing to compare in scale. Euston, for example, has only fifteen platforms to Grand Central's forty-four."

Lord Tallis's discourse was interrupted by the arrival of Partridge, who was followed closely by a footman pushing a large tea trolley and two maids bearing various other items.

When the necessary fussing around with tea cup and plates was complete, and the four servants had withdrawn, Tallis brought the meeting to order.

"Now, Inspector, give us whatever news you can. I gather you arrested this Saunders woman yesterday; hopefully you've gleaned something from her? I'm quite resigned, by the way, to hearing that one of my sons-in-law is a murderer. The floor is yours."

"Thank you, my lord. I'm pleased to tell you that neither Mr Carey nor Mr Starling is a murderer, although as Mr Hammond has no doubt explained, both men appear to be guilty of various lesser matters."

The DI's three listeners all looked surprised. "Lost the mental bet I placed, then," interjected Meredith Hammond.

"From what Miss Saunders told me, this is what happened. I believe her, incidentally. Mr Carey invited her to this house, allegedly following your advice, m'lord. Not long afterwards, she mentioned this invitation to another of her clients, Bruce Leach."

There was a collective intake of breath from the other men in the room. "Ah," said Tallis with a satisfied look on his face. "Sorry, Inspector, do carry on."

"She only told him because she was aware that his father was a peer, and she would be visiting the house of another. Leach displayed keen interest in this, and asked a lot of questions. It would seem that he became very indiscreet. Saunders says that he told her he needed to get some of what he called 'his' papers out of your safe, m'lord, although he didn't explain what these were.

"He also told her of a remarkable coincidence – that he too was to be a guest in this house at the same time.

"During the following conversation Cissie Saunders, who admits that she was infatuated with the man, boasted that she knew someone who specialised in opening safes. I don't know all the details yet, and they don't really matter anyway. Suffice it to say that Danny Skinner was recruited to crack the safe. No doubt Leach provided the information telling him how many windows along the terrace he needed to count to reach the study.

"Saunders denies that she had any inkling that Leach intended to kill Skinner. That may be true – she'd known him for years and he'd been something like an uncle to her while she was a child. However, it's a fact that she didn't immediately denounce Leach the next morning."

"That's right, Inspector," said Walter Tallis. "She was as cool as a cucumber, as I recall."

"Well, m'lord, so far I've only charged her with conspiracy to commit burglary. Her statement effectively admits that matter. But my superiors will no doubt consider other charges, perhaps being an accessory before the fact to an act or murder. If so, the evidence from those present that morning may well be crucial.

"The connection between Leach and Saunders explains something which puzzled me earlier. Mr Carey brought the woman here quite brazenly, and Mrs Carey even thought that her husband had intended to pay a visit to Cissie's room that night. But then there suddenly seemed to be a cooling in the relationship. Cissie explained to me that Mr Carey found out that evening that she knew Leach – and that he was one of her clients. He didn't like it.

"Anyway, to bring you all up to date. A few minutes before I left to come here, I heard that Mr Leach has been arrested by officers from the Metropolitan Police, on suspicion of murder. He is being brought up here, and I expect to interview him this evening.

"I have to say, m'lord, that without your generosity, and Mr Hammond's help in organising his agents, we'd never have got this far. I'm sure Colonel Meadows will pass on the constabulary's appreciation more formally."

"Forget it, Inspector. But you made one mistake in your report. You referred to Leach's attendance as a remarkable coincidence. It wasn't entirely coincidental. You see, I was already aware of the Saunders woman's existence. I anticipated that when I more or less told Carey to invite some unlikely person that he would quite probably choose his current paramour. He thought she'd given up the game, but then he's always been naïve.

"My aim, discreditable though it may have been, was to bring the actions of Carey and Starling into the open in some way, perhaps by precipitating a number of rows during the visit. As Meredith will have told you, I've had Leach's father in my sights for some time.

"So, I actually asked Charity to invite young Leach. In loyalty to me she didn't tell you that, and she asks me to pass on her apologies. Of course, until just now I had no idea that he was also linked to the prostitute.

"Frankly, I had no real plan beyond getting these people together; I just hoped to bring a lot of things into the open, and I wanted to do it face-to-face as far as possible.

"Then, of course, I was called away, and it was really too late to change the arrangements. I apologise to you, Walter, because I ruined your celebration; my only excuse is that if I'd succeeded in my crude plan, several people would be happy – including your two younger sisters who would almost certainly have got rid of the husbands that both now regret marrying.

"I knew that Angus Leach would have told his son that I'd been investigating his affairs. I have always been aware that the documents in my safe were at risk. If young Leach was in the house, it would have been an opportunity for him which might never recur. The same was true of my sons-in-law too. I didn't know how any one of them might get access to the safe, or even if they would try. But it seems my hunch was right. The thing I couldn't have anticipated, of course, was that the man brought in to open the safe would be killed. I still don't understand why that was necessary."

"I rather think it was a matter of Leach's

security, Edgar," said Hammond. He was aware that Cissie came from a family of criminals, and I suspect he feared that Skinner would blab to them. Word would get around, and that could mean blackmail, or even worse, the police hearing about it. Skinner had to be eliminated."

"I agree," said Rees. "I'd go further. I think he decided that Cissie would have to go too. Even if Cissie had told anyone, her father, say, if she and Skinner were both dead there was no evidence against him. Two nights ago Cissie was almost killed when a car swerved off the road. It was a miracle that it missed her – and the driver didn't stop. She hadn't connected the incident with Wythall, and only mentioned it to me during the interview because, as she said, it had shaken her up. But as soon as I suggested it was deliberate she visibly paled. It seems after the murder she never had an opportunity to speak to Leach alone, so she hadn't asked him why he'd killed Skinner. She not entirely stupid, and as soon as I floated the idea she accepted at once that she would be next."

"I told you that Angus Leach is about the most obnoxious man I've ever met, Inspector," remarked Hammond. "It would appear that his son is no better."

"Well, Inspector, we can't go much further today. Presumably there will be an inquest very soon. I suppose I may be involved, to testify about the safe contents. I'd be obliged if you'll let us know when Leach is charged. Let me just explain, for your ears only, my position regarding the other matters.

"Details of the offences committed by my sons-in-law will be given to the police in Birmingham and London tomorrow. I rather think that the provenance of the information will ensure that the matters are taken seriously. I have explained the situation to my two younger daughters, who are, as I implied before, not unhappy. For the sake of their children, though, no doubt they'll be glad that neither of their husbands is to be hanged.

"Also tomorrow, the dossier on Angus Leach will be passed to the Metropolitan Police Commissioner in person. Again, coming from me, no cover-up will be permitted. I expect Leach to be arraigned before our fellow-peers within two or three months. It'll be only the third trial of a peer in the House this century. I may well be a witness, but even if I am not, I certainly won't exercise my right to vote."

CHAPTER 22

Rees sang some more on his way back to the police station. After what even he accepted was an excruciating rendition of one of the songs from The Merry Widow, as performed by Maurice Chevalier, he rested his vocal cords for the remainder of the journey.

He worked silently at his desk for the next ninety minutes. Everyone else in the office had gone home, although Knowles was due to return later to assist in Leach's interview. The DI was suddenly interrupted by the unprecedented arrival of the Chief Constable, who coughed gently to announce his presence. It took a minute for Rees to recover, but Colonel Meadows was clearly a happy man, and told the DI to sit down again, and perched himself on a very tatty chair nearby.

"Edgar Tallis tells me that you've given him the latest facts, Rees, and that everything is fine from his point of view. Well done, man."

"That's so sir. But as I said to his lordship, we couldn't have done without his finance, and your godson's help. I hope you'll put that more formally, sir."

"Oh yes, certainly. There will be an official letter of thanks going out tomorrow. Now, I understand you're expecting this Leach man this evening. Do you have enough to hold him?"

"Not only to hold him, sir; I expect to charge him."

"Excellent. Carry on then, Inspector."

The Chief Constable disappeared almost as quickly as he had arrived, and Rees returned to his paperwork. Another twenty minutes had passed when the Custody Sergeant poked his head around the door and announced that two London officers had just delivered Bruce Leach.

"I've stuck him in a cell for the moment, sir, but he's asking for a solicitor."

"Has he named a particular one?"

"No; he says anyone will do, just to get him out of here!"

"Fine; get him someone who can be here in the next half hour. But Leach leaves here tonight over my dead body!" Rees went out with the Sergeant to thank the Met officers for delivering their prisoner.

Knowles arrived a few minutes later, and Rees explained there would be a delay. However, far quicker than expected, the desk man came in again.

"It happened that Mr Pike was in the station seeing a client, sir, and he agreed to talk to Leach. Seems he was deemed suitable, and they're ready for you now. They're in the interview room."

The DI and Sergeant Knowles joined the other two. Both officers knew the wily old Solicitor well, and of course both had met Leach before. Rees opened the proceedings.

"You've been arrested on suspicion of murder, Mr Leach, and you have been told that you don't have to say anything, and warned that anything you do say will be noted and may be used in evidence."

Mr Pike spoke. "My client instructs me that he knows nothing of this murder, and that in due course he will sue this constabulary for wrongful arrest. I understand there is no evidence against him to hold him on any matter. I need hardly add that he is a man of impeccable character. I have advised him not to answer any questions. However, as he believes it will expedite his release, he has chosen to answer your questions. I shall, of course, give him further advice if appropriate."

"Thank you. Now, Mr Leach, you accept, do you not, that some of the documents taken from Lord Tallis's safe contained information about your father which was potentially very damaging?"

"I have not seen these alleged documents, so I cannot comment on their content."

"You admitted earlier that you knew enquiries had been made, but we won't quibble. Anyway, let me assist you. As I told you the other day, all the documents were duplicated, and I have now been able to see them. I can confirm that the documents relating to your father are of two distinct types. First, those detailing the purchase of his barony. I imagine the publication of those would be highly embarrassing to both your father and you. However, the police are not concerned with that, as no offence was committed at the time.

"The second set concerns a number of criminal matters, and no doubt of more urgent concern to your father. And, indirectly, to you. The offences – described in considerable detail, with witness statements and so on – are such that your father is looking at spending at least ten years as an unwilling guest of His Majesty.

"So your motive for acquiring – and then destroying – these documents is quite clear."

"You say so, Inspector. But you presuppose that I was aware that these documents were in the safe. I wasn't, and you cannot prove that I was. You also seem to be implying that I killed the man who apparently broke into that safe. You cannot prove that either. Indeed, if I had wanted to take these documents, why should I kill the man who helped me to acquire them?"

"Oh, I think that's obvious. You couldn't possibly take the risk that Skinner would talk about the job. Much better to eliminate him as soon as he'd opened the safe. Perhaps he even looked at the papers before handing them to you."

"Tommyrot," commented Leach. "How much longer are you intending to keep me here?"

"We have a bed for you overnight, Mr Leach. But you won't be going anywhere, ever. Unless you count the journey to Winson Green. In due course, that's where you'll be hanged. By that time, your father will be in prison too. Unfortunately, he'll probably be in Pentonville, otherwise he could have heard the trapdoor opening under you."

Leach glared at Rees without speaking. Mr Pike, who was looking horrified, remonstrated with the DI. "You shouldn't say things like that, Inspector; not the thing at all."

"You're entitled to your view, Mr Pike; I'm entitled to mine. Let's move on. When I interviewed you at Wythall, Mr Leach, you said you had never met Cissie Saunders before."

"That's right. I don't say I might not have seen her somewhere in London – I'm often around the West End – but if so I don't recall it."

"Not a very wise denial, Mr Leach. As I told you all in the dining room at Wythall, detectives had also been checking on Miss Saunders. Quite incidental to the main purpose of those checks, which was her relationship with Norman Carey, the names of three of her other upmarket clients were obtained and recorded. Yours was one. We know of at least four occasions when you went with her to a hotel – and of course we have witnesses. Why did you deny knowing her?"

Leach hesitated. "Obviously, I didn't want anyone to know that I'd been with a prostitute."

"Come now, Mr Leach, that's hardly persuasive. No skin off your nose for us to know. You are a single man without ties. We were investigating a murder. The police would never broadcast what you told us.

"No; you didn't want your acquaintance with Cissie to come out for quite a different reason. You learned that she came from a family with many criminal connections – and you wanted to find a safebreaker. And Cissie provided that person."

"If she did, it was for Carey – she works for him and they're obviously very close."

The Inspector shook his head slowly. "I don't think so," he said. "During our first interview at Wythall, when I asked if you knew a Danny Skinner, you said the name didn't ring any bells – and that if that was the burglar you didn't move in those circles."

Leach looked a little wary now, but with a smile confirmed that what he'd said at the time was correct.

"That's a bit strange, Mr Leach, because my information is rather different. I know that you met Skinner in a pub in Albany Street – The Queens Head and Artichoke. Neutral ground, as it were, as it's some way from both your home and his. You stayed there together, drinking and talking, for the best part of two hours. What do you say about that?"

"I say this – what witnesses?"

"I'm sure you know the answer to that, Mr Leach. The principal witness is the other person you initially denied knowing at all – Cissie

Saunders. She has made a very full statement, which includes the fact that she set up the meeting at your request, as you'd asked her if she knew a safebreaker. Enquiries are in train to find others who saw you and Skinner together that evening. It's only a few weeks ago, so we're very hopeful. Not that corroboration is necessary.

"Enquiries are also being made about the pistol, and the silencer. Again, we're confident. But Cissie's statement, and the lies you've told about not knowing either her or Skinner, will be quite sufficient to convict you.

"Oh, just one other thing. There was an attempt on Miss Saunder's life a couple of days ago. We're looking to see if you were responsible for that, too.

"Would you care to make a formal statement now?"

The Solicitor leaned forward and shook his head firmly. My advice is to say nothing more, Mr Leach. I wish you had heeded my advice earlier."

Leach nodded slowly. "Right."

Rees stood up. "Bruce Leach, I charge you with conspiring with Daniel Skinner to commit an act of burglary, contrary to the Larceny Act. I also charge you with the murder of Daniel Skinner, contrary to the Common Law.

Leach looked down at the table in front of him, and said nothing.

"Take him away, Sergeant, and get him booked in properly."

The Solicitor looked gloomily at Rees when his client had left the room. "You're pretty confident, then?"

"Oh yes. Cissie will make a very good witness. And his lies will destroy his own credibility."

"Has she been charged?"

"Although she arranged the meeting in the public house, she wasn't present, and in theory doesn't know what was discussed. It's a moot point as to whether she knew that the intention was to kill Skinner, but she certainly didn't immediately denounce Leach when the body was found. Anyway, I haven't charged her with anything relating to the murder. I've only charged her with conspiracy to commit an act of burglary. She appeared before the magistrates this morning, and was remanded in custody.

"Someone higher up the chain will decide whether to charge her with the far more serious matter of being an accessory before the fact. I think it's very unlikely, though. The principle of King's Evidence would no doubt be raised to save her from the gallows. And, as you'll know better than I do, her evidence would then need more corroboration than if she were just an ordinary witness. Anyway, I think she genuinely didn't know; and when she found out, simply didn't know what to do."

Pike nodded sadly. "No doubt Lord Leach will have his own solicitor when he's arrested, but I suppose he might suggest his counsel also defends the son; there wouldn't seem to be a conflict of interest."

"No, replied, the DI, "but of course they won't be tried together. His Lordship's case isn't my business, which is a pity – it isn't every day there's a trial in the House of Lords, and I'm never likely to see another!"

The Solicitor smiled. "No," he agreed. "But suppose they had been charged together, with an identical offence, and would normally have been side by side in the same dock. Interesting legal point – would the son get to be tried alongside his father by the Lords, or would the father be tried with his son at the Assizes – or would the cases be separated?"

"No precedent for that scenario, I imagine," replied the DI. "The whole 'tried by his peers' thing is somewhat absurd anyway."

When Pike had gone, Rees walked up to his office, and picked up the telephone. "Get me Lord Tallis at Wythall, Maudie," he instructed the switchboard operator.

****

BOOKS BY THIS AUTHOR

The Bedroom Window Murder

It is 1949. Sir Francis Sherwood – WW1 hero, landowner, magistrate – is shot dead while standing at an open bedroom window in his country house. A rifle is found in the grounds.

The county police seek help from Scotland Yard.

Detective Chief Inspector Bryce and Detective Sergeant Haig are assigned to the case. The first difficulty for the Yard men is that nobody with even a mild dislike of Sherwood can be found.

But before that problem can be resolved, others arise...

The Courthouse Murder

In July 1949, an unpopular and deeply unpleasant man is stabbed in the courthouse of an English city. As the murder has been committed in a room to which the general public doesn't have access, it seems probable that the culprit is someone involved with the business of the courts.

Suspects include a number of lawyers, police officers, and magistrates.

For various reasons, the local Chief Constable decides to ask Scotland Yard to investigate the murder.

Chief Inspector Philip Bryce and Sergeant Alex Haig are assigned to the case.

Theirs is a recent partnership, but the two men worked well together in another murder case a few weeks before. (See 'The Bedroom Window Murder'.)

The Felixstowe Murder

In August 1949, Detective Chief Inspector Bryce and his new bride are holidaying in the East Anglian seaside resort of Felixstowe.

During afternoon tea in the Palm Court of their hotel, a man dies at a nearby table.

Reluctant to get directly involved, Bryce nevertheless agrees to help the inexperienced local police inspector get to grips with his first murder case, turning his own honeymoon into a 'busman's holiday'.

Multiples Of Murder

Three more cases for Philip Bryce. The first two are set in 1949, and follow on from The Bedroom Window Murder, The Courthouse Murder, and The Felixstowe Murder.
The third goes back to 1946, when Bryce – not long back in the police after his army service – was a mere Detective Inspector, based in Whitechapel rather than Scotland Yard.

1. In the office kitchen of a small advertising agency in London, a man falls to the floor, dead. Initially, it is believed that he had some sort of heart attack, but it soon becomes clear that he had received a fatal electric shock. A faulty kettle is then blamed. But evidence emerges showing that this was not an accident. Chief Inspector Bryce is assigned to the case.

2. Just before opening time, a body is found in the larger pool at the huge public baths in St Marylebone. The man has been shot, presumably the previous evening. It is DCI Bryce's task, aided by Detective Sergeant Haig and others, to discover the identity of the victim, why he was killed, and who shot him.

3. For a few months in 1946, a traditional London bus was modified in an experiment to allow passengers to 'Pay-As-You-Board'. Doors were fitted, instead of having the usual open platform. The stairs rose from inside the saloon rather than directly from the platform. On the upper deck, a man is found stabbed to death. None of the passengers can shed any light on the murder, yet the design of this bus meant that no-one could have jumped off the bus unnoticed – one of them must be the murderer. Inspector Bryce, together with colleagues from Leman Street police station, solves one of his earlier cases.

Death At Mistram Manor

In September 1949, a wake is being held at a manor house in Oxfordshire, following the burial of the chatelaine. Over a hundred mourners are present.

Within an hour, the clergyman who conducted the funeral service is taken ill himself. The local doctor, present at the wake, provisionally diagnoses appendicitis, and calls for an ambulance. However, the priest dies soon after being admitted to hospital.

An autopsy reveals that the cause of death was strychnine poisoning.

The circumstances are such that accidental ingestion and suicide are both ruled out. The rector was murdered, and the timing means that the poison must have been taken during the wake.

The local police, faced with a lengthy list of potential suspects, ask Scotland Yard to take on the investigation, and the case is assigned to Detective Chief Inspector Bryce and two colleagues.

Although most of the mourners can easily be eliminated from the enquiry, around eight of them cannot. The experienced London officers have to sift through a number of initially-promising indications, before finally being able to identify the killer.

Machinatiions Of A Murderer

There are at least two reasons why Robin Whitaker wants to eliminate his wife, Dulcie. He is not allowed to drink any alcohol, nor to gamble.

Dulcie controls his life to an extent that he finds intolerable. But she is also wealthy, so merely leaving her is not an acceptable option.

In most circumstances Dr Whitaker thinks and acts like the very intelligent and highly-educated man he is. However, he has somehow convinced himself that the action of killing his wife is justified. He is also certain that his innate brainpower will give him a significant edge over any police detectives, and allow him to outwit them with ease.

What are his thoughts? How does he make his decisions? What does he do?

Will he get away with murder?

Suspicions Of A Parlourmaid; The Norfolk Railway Murders

Two more cases for Philip Bryce.

1 An affluent elderly lady dies. The death certificate cites 'natural causes', but the servants are uncomfortable.

A parlourmaid decides to go to New Scotland Yard, and talk to someone there. She is fortunate, because Detective Sergeant Haig happens to pass through the foyer while she is explaining. The busy desk officer intercepts him, and asks to him to listen to the maid's story.

Haig listens politely, but is ready to dismiss the story as tittle-tattle, when he hears one thing which makes him take notice. He goes to report to his boss, DCI Bryce, who also finds the point of interest, and speaks to the maid himself.

The full might of the Metropolitan Police is then focused on the matter – and a post mortem examination reveals that the lady certainly did not die from natural causes.

In the leafy South London suburb of Dulwich Village, Bryce and Haig investigate the happenings, and sort out who is innocent, and who is guilty.

2. DCI Bryce is sent to Norfolk, where two solicitors have been killed. There are obvious connections between the crimes. First, both men were partners in the same firm. But also, both appeared to have been killed while travelling on local railway trains, and the bodies then thrown off. Over the whole existence of railways in Britain, the number of such cases could be counted on the fingers of one hand. So one such case would have been rare enough, but for there to be two – on different trains and a few days apart – was almost unbelievable.

However, shortly before these two men were found, a third body was discovered. This victim didn't seem to have any connection to the firm of solicitors – but he too was found beside a railway track.

A temporary absence of CID officers in King's Lynn causes the Chief Constable to ask Scotland Yard to take the case. DCI Bryce and two of his officers travel to West Norfolk, where they find a local Detective Constable eager to help.

Which of the three victims was the real target, and which murders were either dry runs or red herrings?

This Village Is Cursed

A young provincial journalist receives a telephone call from a man who won't give his name. Anticipating the scoop of his career, Marcus Cunningham arranges to meet the informant at Liverpool Street station.

Subsequent events quickly draw in Scotland Yard detectives Chief Inspector Philip Bryce and his colleague Sergeant Alex Haig, as they conduct a complex murder investigation.

The Amateur Detective

In 1950, a death occurs under the uniquely-banded cliffs in Hunstanton. It is soon realised that this is a case of murder, but the Norfolk police inspector runs into difficulties, and Scotland Yard

DCI Philip Bryce finds himself back in the county for the second time in a matter of months.

A local amateur detective with a considerable knowledge of murder cases (both real and fictional) is determined to help the police, and comes up with various suggestions. However, initially neither he nor the police seem to be able to pin all the usual key elements – means, motive, and opportunity – on any one person.

With the possible list of suspects narrowed down to relations of the deceased and a group of bridge-playing friends, will the amateur measure up to the standards of sleuthing shown by his fictional heroes, and solve the case ahead of the professionals?

Eventually, one person ends up in the dock at the Assizes in Norwich – but the drama still hasn't ended!

Demands With Menaces

1950. Out of the blue, Philip Bryce is suddenly given two pieces of news – one domestic, the other work-related.

Within hours, he finds himself given a 'double-jump' promotion, and put in charge of a new and important department at Scotland Yard.

At the same time he learns about his promotion, he is given a new case. It's a change from the murder cases he spends a lot of time on, but it's tricky. This one involves 'demands with menaces' – blackmail. And the first three victims are high-ranking people – a rich peer, a government minister, and a bishop. In fact so important are they that the Commissioner instructs the newly appointed Detective Chief Superintendent to take charge of the case himself.

Bryce investigates, with the also-promoted Inspector Haig alongside him.

But who is the blackmailer? From where does he or she acquire the information? And just how innocent are the 'victims'?

Printed in Great Britain
by Amazon